Also available soon from Indigo Sea Press
by Dene Hellman

The People Under the House

indigoseapress.com

Critical Praise for "The Ninety-Ninth Reunion"

Two sisters attend the 99th annual reunion at an Iowa school. Maggie, the younger one, is a psychic and has some foreboding about the return. She is right in her apprehensions. At the reunion and during the weeks that follow, emotions are stirred, a ghost is sensed, a farmhouse burns, and tragedy sweeps the countryside. Hellman ties up all the ends of this intriguing story with skill and insight. The result is a very good read.

I highly recommend *The 99th Reunion* to those who have attended a high school reunion or who intend to do so!

—**Hughlett L. Morris**, author of *The Cass Street Kid*

The story of *The 99th Reunion* is told through several voices – a dyslexic psychic, an Iowa farmer with a calling to protect the environment, a corporate communications woman back in Iowa after years of living in the South, and a sociopathic retired teacher relentlessly pursuing her own interests. Each voice is distinct and fully captured my interest. A white convertible named 'Max," is a sort of white light bridge that connects the past with the present. These components, plus a surprise ending, wrung my emotions until I was delightfully exhausted. More, please!

—**Ann Marie O'Dell**, *Achieve* Radio Host

As a native Iowan, I've grown accustomed to the world's frequent perceptions of the Midwest as a Grant Wood sea of bucolic fields, punctuated by picturesque towns with double-digit populations of simple but decent people who talk about the weather, worry about the state fair, and live their lives from one Sunday supper to the next.

Dene Hellman does a fine job playing with rural America stereotypes in *The 99th Reunion*. Or, perhaps, she plays with our expectations through an efficient and polished prism of first-person perspectives!

Ratchford, Iowa's 99th reunion is merely the small-town petri dish for Hellman's experiment, a place where folks who knew your grandfather's cousin's sister get up and leave town, return, go about their business while watching and, often, judging one another's lives, pies, and murder. It is a place where the loudest opinions are rarely spoken – but Hellman makes sure we hear every word.

Sisters Maggie and Janilee Jaspers' return to their rural hometown is a deceptive façade for the reader's journey, much as Maggie's psychic talents may be a warm-up for the subjective narrative lenses that Hellman efficiently puts on the reader. As quickly as we are drawn into Maggie's head, we learn this is no tale of sisterly bonding. Cleverly, Hellman uses Maggie's sixth sense to accelerate our introductions to Ratchford's interconnected cast of characters.

The shift from Maggie's free-spirited and calm worldview to Lee's meticulous measurements of past, present and future is brilliantly jarring. For Lee, a road trip that began as a whimsical venture is suddenly a passionate, whirlwind, made-for-each-other love—albeit one with a business plan. For her, Ben Deckard, a valedictorian farm boy, is unfinished business. Now, the charming, educated, moneyed and eco-friendly Ben seems to be everything she needs to swim out of a stagnant passage in her life. And when Hellman's focus tracks to Ben's voice, even his romantic reflection on his perpetual crush on Lee cites her as an "incredible asset" to his life as he wishes to live it.

In retrospect, the portrayal of Lee's and Ben's passion is a clever setup for our shocking fourth narrator, a retired teacher who knows them all. A self-proclaimed "chosen image of superior womanhood," she recounts a life of diabolical machinations, assembling a dark puzzle that brings everything together.

The 99th Reunion is a page-turner of literary optical illusion; no matter what lens Hellman has us peering through, she is discreetly connecting dots we won't notice until the gathered clues pounce from the page in a series of escalating zingers.

—**Paul P. Soucek**, *Earshot Sound Technology*, Los Angeles

I enjoyed *The 99th Reunion* to the point of irritating my family! They said to me, "Can't you read more quietly, without chuckling and laughing out loud so much?"

I could not. I'd grown up in a town like the one brought to life in this book and really enjoyed reminiscing about the Ratchford people and events. It was a most enjoyable read!

—**Marcia Meis**, Native Iowan

The Ninety-Ninth Reunion

By

Dene Hellman

Deep Indigo Books
Published by Indigo Sea Press
Winston-Salem

Deep Indigo Books
Indigo Sea Press
302 Ricks Drive
Winston-Salem, NC 27103

First Deep Indigo Books edition published
December, 2015
Deep Indigo Books, Moon Sailor and all production design are trademarks of Indigo Sea Press, used under license.

For information regarding bulk purchases of this book, digital purchase and special discounts, please contact the publisher at indigoseapress.com

Cover design by Stacy Castanedo

Manufactured in the United States of America
ISBN 978-1-63066-245-5

For a quartet

of wonderful daughters:

Ann Marie, Jean, Katherine, and Patricia

Acknowledgments

Nearly every author whose book is barely out of the gestation stage looks for affirmation.

It then falls to a chosen "First Reader" to tread the sticky ground between "Go!" and "You may want to rethink this—or this—or this." I was fortunate in my choice of "First Reader" and owe a tremendous debt of gratitude to that person for enthusiastic encouragement as well as some well-placed and tactful suggestions.

As *The Ninety-Ninth Reunion* went through its several adjustments, others—including Hughlett Morris and Kenneth Youngblood—contributed important suggestions and encouragement and I thank them. Grandson Patrick Bartholomew was also vastly helpful. Since he seemingly was in the self-imposed process of reading every book ever written, I asked him to take time off to read what I considered my finished manuscript. When I grilled him later, he was forthcoming about what he liked, didn't like, and sometimes found insufficiently clear. Back to the computer I went and Patrick will read the revised copy while on duty in Afghanistan. I hope he approves. Special thanks go to Annie O'Dell, who was the source of information about how psychics (or, as she would call them, "intuitives") do their jobs.

Mike Simpson of Second Wind Publishers is greatly appreciated for his open-minded approach to new manuscripts and I thank him. This is a time when too many publishers are chiefly interested in books by (often by ghost writers) the latest people involved in a scandal, crime or titillating circumstance. Indigo Sea Press doesn't fall into that group. May it live long and prosper!

Book One: The Psychic

One

IF I SHOULD HAVE TO PLACE SOMETHING or someone at the center of what happened, I would be tempted to jab a finger straight at one of Max's aggressive little fog lights.

Max is the white Chrysler convertible I bought third-hand from a woman who had gone up in the world and now would only drive new. Max wasn't shabby. His black interior was flawless. He had been kept garaged and polished to a sheen that glinted off his former mistress's highlighted red hair like sunlight on a hotel swimming pool. He wasn't even all that old—maybe six years.

Being deeded over to me was surely a comedown for Max. Going to stay in a small Wisconsin town and then getting housed in a detached out-building that was more tool shed than garage was bad enough. Having a magnetic sign clapped on each door that announced "Intuitive Counseling: Maggie's Serene Sanctuary" was certainly not equal in status to being eased into a reserved parking place at a Madison hospital to await the emergence of a white-coated Catch-of-the-Day. I knew it and Max must have felt it clear down to his exquisite suspension parts.

No auto owner could have been more delighted with a new acquisition than I was. After 10 years of hard work developing a reputation as a genuinely talented and caring psychic, I was ready to promote myself from the rust-bucket all-terrain vehicles I use to haul around the dogs to the self-appointed reward of a flashy car.

Did I mention that the convertible's name, Max, is short for "Maximum Freedom?" I had visions of driving happily into the wind with my ash blonde hair streaming behind, headed for some glorious adventure that had nothing to do with veterinarians or grocery shopping.

I couldn't wait to tell my big sister, Janilee, about my new toy,

remembering, of course, to call Janilee by the shorter name—"Lee."
She adopted that moniker as soon as she could pull it off, which
would have been thirty plus years ago, after she got out of the house
and out from under the censoring thumbs of our mother and step-
father.

"Maggie, be careful," she said, when I bragged about Max.
"Otherwise, good for you! If I could ever find time for anything
besides going to work and keeping up the garden, I'd love to have
some exciting wheels under me!"

That's my sister for you. "If only......If only......." Lee, nine
years older than me, is almost a different generation. When she
graduated from high school back in Ratchford, Iowa, dress codes and
drugs and protest statements had hardly made a visible dent on that
motionless little burg.

Our mother had sent her to grade school in pinafores and pixie
cuts, to be updated later to the most fetching junior-size frocks that
Younkers Department Store in Des Moines could yield. She always
looked too fancy, as her classmates often let her know. Most of the
girls wore blue jeans to school by then, which was appropriate garb
for a farm community. Of course, everybody still dressed up for
church, but no more than necessary. Mother was blissfully unaware
of all that and little Janilee didn't much care. She was on the cusp of
a life-long love affair with clothes and wouldn't have traded her little
Empire-style dresses for a made-in-Home Economics-class skirt for
all the tea in China.

By the time I graduated, our father had died, our mother had
remarried, and we had long since moved to Madison where funky
clothes, designer drugs and a well-deserved reputation for being
Protest City had been in full swing for quite a while.

It didn't take long for Mother to give me up as a hopeless case,
reluctantly getting the message that I didn't even appreciate so-called
"designer" jeans. She'd come home from the shopping mall with
denims that had somebody's fancy name on the back pocket and I'd
ignore them in favor of a ratty pair I'd found in St. Vincent's or
Goodwill.

"Don't you *care* about your appearance?" she would wail at me,
and I'd maybe give her a little hug before walking away to do my
own thing. She meant well but I couldn't share her belief that clothes
were the pivot of life itself.

In a way, Lee and I were polar opposites. If, these days, she felt obligated to caution me to be careful, I felt the same obligation toward her. Which one of us carried the greatest stigmata of worldly experience was a basis for mutual exchanges. I suppose both of us had to learn a lot of things the hard way.

Consider:

Lee had gone from high school to college. I hated school and after graduating had immediately consorted with counter-culture friends, the more dropped-out, the better.

Lee was married by 21 and produced two sons in nearly indecent haste. I bummed around the country, working in factories and flipping Tarot cards in barrooms. I lived with one guy or another for about ten years, thank heaven having the sense not to get married. Actually, I wasn't as attached to any of them as I was to the fact that they represented a certain amount of freedom to come and go as I pleased.

Lee's kids were grown when she was in her early forties and by that time she had a pretty good job as a corporate trainer in a financial company down in the Carolinas and lived in one of those snotty gated communities that keep out the natives. I married Jack after a lengthy recess from my not-so-wonderful relationships and settled down in small-town Wisconsin with a house and yard filled with three dogs, four cats, and the aforementioned rusty four-wheelers.

Lee's husband, Arthur, developed a nasty, no-way-out condition that left him very sick, then dying, then dead, right about the time I got married.

"Be careful," Lee said to me when she came up to Wisconsin to stand up with me at my wedding. "Make sure Jack feels as much responsibility for you as you do for him."

"Be careful," I said to Lee when she obsessed about getting ahead in her job and paying off the debts run up during Arthur's sickness. "You gave him everything you had when he was alive. You owe yourself something now."

"Be careful," Lee said to me when I decided to quit my day job and become a full-time psychic. "Working from home requires more self-discipline than most people can handle."

"Be careful," I said to Lee. "Don't keep turning guys down because you're afraid of making a mistake."

Why she was so particular was sort of puzzling to me. Arthur hadn't been such a great spouse that he was an impossible act to follow. Personally, I had found him lacking in motivation and awareness, not to mention humor. It was sad that he took a long time to die and left Lee with more problems to settle than were balanced by the good stuff. It was her business, however; I tried to stay tactful and concentrate on her future.

But she turned down some pretty cool guys in the following years, guys who would have given her more security and less trauma than she'd ever had. "Oh, Maggie," she would say whenever I questioned her logic. "He and I don't have any of the things in common that I need to have with someone I'd want to hold close in my life."

And, of course, one of the problems was that she was apt to say things like "someone I'd want to hold close in my life." What she really meant was if the guy did not have a degree in Renaissance architecture or play Chopin nocturnes from memory, he was absolutely no candidate for her bedroom.

Which I consider total baloney. It is my contention that a husband can watch the sports channel when you'd rather see a rerun of an old black and white movie, or work on the loading dock while you report to the vice president in charge of marketing. He can pull the lever in the voting booth that cancels out your most sincerely held beliefs—and it still is not a prediction of whether or not you're going to be a pretty happy all-around couple. I try to tell that to people who consult me while boo-hooing about spouses who haven't turned out to be soul mates.

I'm speaking from experience gained as, years back, I finally decided to settle down after more than a decade of bumming around. Before that, I was always finding myself paired up with third-rate musicians or down and out artists or unsuccessful actors—a lot of them looking forward more than anything to their next drink or weed. I evidently had a thing for artistic types and really don't have anything against them now; people are entitled to their dreams. Still, living off somebody else's dreams is pretty unsatisfactory.

When I met Jack, I decided he was really, really cool. He had a little construction business and thought being a good carpenter was the best thing anybody could possibly want. He'd messed up in a marriage he'd had years back, didn't have any kids, and was tired of the single life. Even so, he stayed solvent, minded his own business, and was careful about women.

He and I eyed one another for quite a while before we got

friendly and after we were married we settled down in Boxville, where some of his relatives lived. We thought we'd have kids but it didn't happen and we never tried to figure out whose fault it was. We just naturally started collecting homeless dogs and cats. Both of us worked steady, watched a little TV in the evening after our supper and animal chores were over, and were model citizens. Jack had his sports enthusiasms, which didn't interest me much, and he was less than interested in my psychic business. We never voted for the same people but only rarely had a loud discussion about our political differences.

Lee wasn't even talking about differences *that* extreme. I'd met a few of her would-be suitors over the last few years, even read their palms and dealt the cards. Most of them knew how to hold a knife and fork and had a pretty good idea of what was politically correct.

"This is a good one," I'd say to her. "Hold on to him." The trouble was, she was the only person I knew, outside of Jack, who would not take my intuitive talents seriously. She'd laugh and turn away and two weeks later she wouldn't be returning the guy's phone calls.

Two

SINCE LEE WAS GROWN UP and away from home by the time I was in high school in Madison, there was no reason for her to respect my psychic gifts. Even I had had a hard time understanding what went on in my head.

To say I had a wandering mind when I was in grade school would be an understatement. It was a wonder I learned to read, write and do basic math. Mother would shake her head, year after year, wishing me smarter, wishing I would stop daydreaming.

Daydreaming was not really what I did. There were just so many things going on behind the up-front things that I couldn't concentrate. Instead of listening and learning, I'd be picking up on all kinds of vibrations that sort of buzzed around my teachers and the other kids. I couldn't make sense of it, but by junior high it had gotten to be a kind of game I played by myself. Somebody would be giving a perfectly serious report and some invisible aura hovering in the air around them would make me burst out laughing. Or the assistant principal would stop by to pick up the attendance roster and I'd find myself anxious about what he really had on his mind when he patted a little girl on the shoulder.

Since Mother was good about helping me with homework and was also very good at bullying teachers who questioned my abilities, I never got held back and I hit high school at the usual age and squeaked through. However, I knew by then that any learning I'd do would have to happen at my own pace, outside school.

Because I wasn't uppity and never competitive, friends were easy to find and keep. Fortunately, I learned not to be constantly "reading" everybody I was with. I was not someone who would be described as "spooky" by others. In fact, as I was developing the foundation for my adult persona, I understood that being a down-to-earth person was a real necessity for getting along in daily life. "Down-to-earth" meant I couldn't always be giving advice and worrying about my friends' lives so I developed the skill of shutting off the intuitive parts of my brain when I was with people I knew.

My high school teachers, however, were an entirely different matter. Since I wasn't aiming for any scholarships or yearning to be an officer of any clubs, it left me free to study them as much as I pleased while they stood in front of the room trying to put across their subject matter.

While I had very little experience with life, I knew enough to catch what was actually going on with the ones I found of interest— sometimes specifically and sometimes as a general state of being. For example, Miss Cooper, the algebra teacher, had a lot working away at her about whether to stay in Madison where her family lived or move out to Idaho where her best friend was running a bed and breakfast. In mid-semester she told us about her plans to move on. But, long before that, I saw the way conflict was almost pulling her in two. I knew it had something to do with a need to stay versus a need to go so I was glad when it all came out that she was going to make a break for it.

Then there was Mrs. Wilkins who taught English literature to juniors and seniors. She was a well put-together little package who had plenty of poise and an ability to shame the class jocks who sneered at old King Lear. I sort of admired her and even regretted that, by looking at her, I could tell that she was fucking somebody who wasn't connected with the wedding ring she wore on her left hand. This was not speculation on my part. I *knew*.

Strangest of all, I began to dread the ancient history classes taught by Mr. Case. He was an efficient, concise reporter of the news as it happened in 500 B.C. Never one for dramatics, he was probably pretty dry listening for anyone who had looked forward to learning about the excitement of times past. Mr. Case had an aura of terrible sadness. Watching, I could see someone wanted to comfort him. There were little hands patting at him all the time. The sadder he was, the more those gentle little hands made an effort to bring him ease. They sure had the opposite effect on me. The more they worked at soothing him, the more uneasy I got.

This wrinkle in my ability to know the hidden parts of my teachers was not one I got any pleasure from at all. And I felt even worse when somebody who knew the Cases personally told me they had lost a little girl in a swimming pool accident a few years before.

A real downside to my kind of teacher watching was that the teachers themselves caught on in some unexplainable way. They knew I was not a good and attentive kind of student who was going to rack up an A in the next exam. They just sensed that I was an expert on what was going on in their heads. Mrs. Wilkins, in particular, was not a fan of mine. I had nothing whatsoever against

Jane Austen's books but she flunked me anyway as having a bad attitude. To this day, I hope her husband caught her with her boyfriend and got custody of all the kids.

Three

AS WE GOT OLDER I tried to tell Lee some of this and, in return, she tried to make me understand what it had been like for her, growing up in a small Iowa town. She would have given anything, she said, to have had a chance to attend a high school like mine where she could have taken Latin and French and learned to play the cello. There was just too much difference, it seemed, between Ratchford and Madison to make for complete comprehension of one another's lifestyles.

The two of us had, we figured out, been like two only children with the same parents. Lee had been my doting baby sitter when our parents wanted a night out but we had totally different interests. Later, when our father died from a sudden heart attack and our mother was trying to pull herself together and get used to having a job, Lee read to me and made me breakfasts and dinners and helped me understand the squiggles that were really letters and numbers.

She was more patient than Mother, and didn't put out the attitude that I was a big disappointment for being slow at picking up on school stuff. By all reports, I'd been a happy-go-lucky, seemingly smart preschooler. When teachers began complaining about my academic abilities after I started kindergarten, Mother was in shock. Everyone in the whole family, she and my father included, had been good students. How did I dare mess up? The news about dyslexia and A.D.D. hadn't, as yet, hit the general public and it wouldn't be common knowledge for a good long time.

Lee had a feel for my problem even though it was undefined. She'd help me draw big, big letters on newspapers and we'd cut them out. Then we'd dance around with them, singing goofy songs.

"Give me an 'M,' Give me an 'M' went one song. 'MMMMaggie! Maggie met a mouse!'

We'd do something like that with numbers, too.

After a couple of years, I started identifying the stuff I saw in schoolbooks and eventually scraped along through my classes, never very good at anything, but good enough so Mother quit trying to teach me stuff at home. I didn't like disappointing her but was relieved when she finally shrugged her shoulders and decided I had inherited some unfortunate traits from my father's side of the family.

9

Lee left home for college when I was nine. I missed her with all my heart, but it seemed as if she forgot about me and then replaced me completely, within a short period of time, with her husband and two boys.

She says that was never the case but, after Mother remarried and we had long since moved to Madison, Lee hardly came to visit at all. She didn't care for our step dad and eventually began to develop a reserved attitude toward Mother. She hardly sees them these days, now that they live in Florida, although I'm positive, responsible person that she is, that she'll be there for Mother if and when she is really needed.

AS THE YEARS PASSED, Lee and I found enough in common to make us close friends as well as sisters. She seemed to get a kick out of my independent ways after I graduated. She knew she'd been looked down on as a stick-in-the-mud all through high school and college and would ask me about my life.

Never having puffed a joint or been casual about sex, she'd back me into a corner whenever she got a chance. "What's it LIKE?" she'd demand.

Sometimes I'd tell her, leaving out the parts when life was so hard I'd have to panhandle for food or run to get away from some weirdo who wanted me to do what he said, no matter what outrageous thing he had in mind.

In later years, even when I was working on a factory line looking after plastic extrusions, I was proud that my big sister dressed up to go to work and got promotions from guys who wore suits. For sure, when I had a real problem or a triumph, Lee was the first one I shared it with—a favor she returned up to a certain point. We may have grown up in two different ways but our sister bond held us together.

After I became a genuine advertised-in-the-phone-book, full-time psychic, I often offered my services to Lee but was turned down 99 percent of the time. Also, whether through a phone conversation or an in-person visit, I couldn't read what was going on with her the way I could with other people. She had a way of deliberately closing her mind to me that was disconcerting and hurt my pride. Maybe, I thought, she'd learned to shield her thoughts from me when we were both girls at home in Ratchford. In some way, she'd likely picked up on my gift of insight and found it uncomfortable.

Later, when we'd talk about what was going on in our lives, being more open than we'd be with anyone else, I'd want to get the cards out and have a look at her future and, BAM, the barricades would come down and I'd be shut out.

"You'd just give me advice from the wild blue yonder," she'd say, "but I have to figure things out my own way, with my own measuring stick."

However, Lee cheered me on most of the time, especially when I got more adventurous with learning new things and testing my abilities. She learned about computers before I did and taught me about spell check and other skills that made life easier for me. She may have been skeptical about my psychic abilities but she never put me down. When I did something daring, like adding a studio office to the house or buying Max, she was downright ecstatic.

Four

WE HATCHED A GRAND SCHEME around Max. Lee was due for a two-week vacation, wasn't enthused about spending it in Florida with Mother and didn't have enough money left over from helping her boys and paying Arthur's old medical bills to do something on a grand scale. I had a little more flexibility than she did, but Jack is a stay at home. He doesn't just prefer his own daily routine; he gets really upset if I change mine very much. He is well aware, however, that time spent with Lee is so important to me that he had better keep his cool about that. Anyway, he likes her in an indulgent, raised-eyebrow kind of way.

Lee and I developed a two-week scenario that involved her flying into Madison and staying in Boxville with me, then the two of us driving Max down to Ratchford, Iowa. Lee had received notice about a Ratchford high school reunion coming up and both of us thought that would make a good time to renew acquaintance with our cousin Emily, who lived in the next town over from Ratchford and had been after us for years to come visit.

I met Lee at the Madison airport and we did what we always do when we get together. We began talking and laughing as if we had been out of communication with the whole human race for months. Not only did we have to catch up on what was currently going on in our lives but, together, everything we saw and everyone we met represented a new adventure. We laughed our way to the airport parking lot.

When Lee saw Max it was love at first sight and she immediately included him in the good-time conspiracy.

"I put the top down just for you," I told her. "If you'll just let your hair down, you will appreciate the gesture. Otherwise, it's going to be a struggle for you to stay dignified."

Lee's hair was the subject of an ongoing argument between us. Possessed of a full blackish-brown mane, she had never permed it and hadn't had it styled in years. She just pulled it up in a school-marmish bun or back in a ponytail.

"Let it down!" I'd say every time I saw her. "You're with me—not kissing up to corporate America or angling for membership in MENSA.

It took Max to finally get through to her. Without even asking, Lee did two things in rapid succession. She climbed into the driver's seat and, before I could manage to hand her the keys, she reached up and pulled the pins out of her hair, letting it fall down all around her face.

"Let's go!" she said.

Since I never enjoyed driving in Madison traffic and was sure to get lost before I got out of town, it was a pleasure to sit back on the passenger side as Lee drove us out to Boxville.

Once there, she settled into the back bedroom. Three of my four cats promptly settled in with her, a tradition they had adopted over several years of her visits. I had to be on the phone and available to my clients so, consequently, the cats were sometimes needy. Lee now had a whole week to dedicate to pampering them, a satisfactory state of affairs she enjoyed and the cats assumed as their right.

She understood that I had a job to do if I was going to keep my clients and my bank account in a positive condition. Over the years, we had worked out a kind of rhythm to her visits. In the morning she would catch up on her reading while I talked to clients. In the afternoons we'd go out and do something fun. In the evenings we'd watch whatever movies Lee had seen that she wanted me to see and that we'd managed to find for rent on the DVD shelves of the Boxville convenience store.

"You have to see this!" she would insist. "The screenplay is pure genius!"

Or the sound track—or the acting—or the theme. Jack would usually be polite and watch with us for a while, rolling his eyes at me when he thought Lee couldn't see him. It wouldn't be long before he'd recall that he had promised to help his brother clean out his fishing camper and he'd be out the door and gone until bedtime.

Sometimes, when she was tired of reading, Lee would slip into my studio, curl up in the ratty old club chair, and listen to me at work with my clients. She said it fascinated her to hear me sounding so professional.

"Maggie, you come off like a damn psychiatrist!" she'd say. "It occurs to me that not one of your customers could do any better if she was paying for problem analysis by someone with a bunch of diplomas on her wall. I acknowledge your gift of intuition, but are you sure you're reading that in the cards?"

She couldn't get over the fact that I didn't cheat by skipping the deck and cutting straight to the heart of the matter. I never did. My business phone would ring and I'd answer. If it was an old client, we'd visit awhile, then I'd shuffle the Tarot deck to see what was going on in his or her life. If it was someone new on the phone, I'd ask for their name, then ask why they'd called. They would lay out their situation, taking their time or not depending upon their finances, then blurt out their big question. I'd shuffle and answer according to what came up.

Although she trusted my integrity, Lee just could not understand that I didn't talk from knowledge of psycho-babble, but from what I saw laid out before me on the table. While a beginning reader uses the Tarot deck like flash cards, an experienced psychic regards them more as television screens and, with emptied mind, channels the thoughts that pop up. It is hard to make lay people understand this.

Client confidence didn't let me give Lee the specifics of the people who called, even when I knew some of their names would make her jaw drop. But I'd sometimes spell out the client's general problem to her, knowing she had already heard my advice and would put two and two together.

"That was exactly what I think you should have told her!" she'd say, as if her judgment was founded on some wellspring of true information that her uneducated little sister couldn't possibly have access to.

There were a few times when she saw me flounder, despite the cards, and I'd explain that some people call and give false information about their situation or lie in other ways that throw off the interaction. She also came to realize that most of those who call are deeply sincere in their need for help and that they could be from any financial background, any country, be of any age, and any occupation. I respected my clients totally and tried to make her understand that.

Some people call psychics because they don't have the money to find long-term psychological advice and need some answers now; others call because they have enough money to consult a trusted psychic about every single decision in front of them and prefer to skip a consulting routine with professional shrinks.

Some people call psychics for the peculiar reason that their occupation or status makes them too vulnerable to seek advice in traditional places. For instance, a clergyman may call because he is helplessly in love with a woman who comes to him for counseling about her marriage. Or a corporate head who thinks he is losing his grip calls because he needs help figuring out how to improve his personal standing with his board of directors, and refuses to consult anything other than the supernatural for guidance.

Actually, it would annoy Lee a lot if she knew that I get attention in quite a few more executive suites than she does. Internationally, by the way.

One of the things that intrigues her is the similarity of the most frequent question on everyone's mind, whether calling from the U.S., England, Australia, or any other location. I'd say more than half of my callers have a version of this question uppermost in their concern.

"How does he (or she) feel about me?"

I've read enough sociology to know there are only a few basic needs that preoccupy the animal brain: getting enough food to keep the physical machinery going, sufficient protection from the elements by way of shelter and body cover, and finding an available orifice to receive or appendage to push the stuff that produces another creature like the original.

To this, some students of humanity add the need for recognition. Maybe it is this recognition desire that fuels the need everybody seems to have to know how the object of their affections regards them. I look at the cards every time the question is asked of me and it is hard for some to hear the answer that comes up. People who hear the opposite of what they want to hear tend to go shopping among psychics until they find one who lies and says the right thing.

It has crossed my mind, as a result of this, that more than just a matter of the natural urge to screw, an undue number of the human race are looking for recognition from someone special for gut reasons that science has not yet worked out. Tap any head of state, world-wide, and I'll bet this is as true as it is for the person who dishes out spaghetti at the local diner in Milwaukee.

So, "How does he feel about me?" is a legitimate question that deserves a serious answer. I regret that Lee thinks it funny.

In recent years, Lee had seemed contented with her experience with guys. In college she'd had enough choices to think she was choosing Arthur. I was too young at the time to be a reliable observer but my later suspicion was that she had picked out the guy who scared her the least. It was a decision that she lived with gracefully, if not joyously, for years without, to my knowledge, doing any cheating. That subject wasn't up for discussion between us, ever.

15

At the same time, Lee had a way of interacting with men, especially after Arthur died, that I found puzzling. She may have reached her middle years, age-wise, but she seemed to show something on her face or in her body language that caused a certain number of the males she encountered to feel disturbed. Especially if she looked at them a second time with her hard and searching gaze, her hazel eyes wide open to possibilities.

I wondered if she even knew she did this. My personal conclusion was that, whether she knew it or not, she was always looking for someone she'd missed meeting but who she knew was waiting for her somewhere.

Five

OUR WEEK IN BOXVILLE was as much fun as always. In years past, Lee had wanted to spend time in Madison strolling State Street and investigating funky second-hand stores but for the last couple of years she seemed to find more pleasure in Wisconsin rural areas. I think she was homesick for the country and didn't know it.

A must was to have lunch as often as possible in Boxville's one restaurant, the Four Corners Café. Since neither of us was much inclined to stringent dieting, we were addicted to Four Corner's butterscotch malts, made with real stuff and dished up in metal containers that filled our glasses again and again.

Jack was always good to grill us brats in the evening and Lee said she liked to time her visits to get in a Wisconsin Friday night fish fry. She had learned all that from visiting me. Iowa had its charms, too, I guess, but even though it was neighboring state to Wisconsin, in some ways they could have been two different countries. Lee said they would be if they were in Europe. If that was the case, when she moved to the Carolinas it must have been like moving from Norway to Italy.

One of the other things she liked to do up north was hit the dress shops in some of the surrounding county seat towns. There is always at least one per town that sells clothes for people who go places where blue jeans and a nice tee fall short of appropriate attire.

Gleaning the sales racks, Lee always said the best things hadn't sold, and the price was unbelievably low for quality clothing. Each summer she could pick up clothes that would carry her through her next corporate fall and winter in Charlotte.

One thing on her mind this trip was what she'd wear to this upcoming ninety-ninth high school reunion event in Ratchford.

"Don't dress up too much," I begged her. "You've always said you and Mother had too much fun dressing you for school and you thought the other kids resented it. Ratchford doesn't have any Southern belles these days, either, I'm sure. And I doubt if they want any."

After trying to gift me with a filmy silk blouse that she said matched my blue eyes, and being turned down flat, Lee settled down and picked out a pair of white jeans that hugged her curves and a

17

green cotton knit top that did very nice things for what she called "the girls." For sure, she'd hung on to the great figure of her earlier years. This time she had my approval about what she picked to wear. At least I wasn't going to have to cringe when I delivered her to her former classmates or when we renewed acquaintance with Cousin Emily. They'd all welcome her back more heartily if they thought her a little bit under-dressed for the occasion.

Max got his own little spruce-up. Jack didn't much care for him, and especially hated driving him when the "Intuitive Counseling" signs were on the doors, but he realized the importance to his wife of a good wash and wax job on her car. Besides, it was his version of a romantic gesture.

"I don't want you taking any chances with safety on this trip," he said. Then he installed four new tires on Max, as well. He was sincere about it but I knew it would cost me camping-out time at Devil's Lake State Park some cold fall weekend, admiring his rock climbing when I'd rather be home brushing the cats.

We were packed and ready Saturday morning when Lee suddenly admitted to cold feet about our plans.

"Why am I doing this?" she demanded. "Nobody down there liked me, and I didn't really like very many of them. If I'd been good at basketball or played the clarinet, I might have felt like part of the place, but studying to get good grades so I could go to college on a scholarship left me out of the loop most of the time. I never knew what to say to anybody and I still don't! I've never gone back to a reunion to this day. Why am I spoiling my record?"

"We don't have to," I said. "We can take Cousin Emily out to dinner and go have a beer."

Rather ridiculously, Lee said, "We have to do the reunion. I paid in advance for our dinners."

The real reason she insisted on going through with this, I thought, was that she'd actually gotten pretty good at people over the years. She had learned how to push her shyness into a dark room in her brain and slam the door. In time, she had developed the skill to work with people, to manage different kinds of projects, even to be a leader of sorts. Probably nobody who had known her over the last twenty-five years guessed how hard it sometimes was for her to deliver an appearance of perfect relaxed poise and self-confidence.

She was most likely forcing herself to go to this reunion to test herself against the hardest set of circumstances she could imagine and there was no way her inner dictator would let her drop the challenge. This was, I thought, going to be an interesting evening of sister-watching.

Then it was my turn to balk. The sight of the map Jack was flourishing sent me into panic. "I don't like driving in strange places," I owned up to Lee. "I especially don't like interstate highways. You're going to have to get behind the wheel."

It was as good as finding a new puppy under the Christmas tree for Lee. She climbed into Max, settled a visored cap on her head and said, just as she had that first day at the Madison airport, "Let's go!"

Jack stood along the driveway looking forlorn and neglected, even though he and his brother had a big weekend of NASCAR watching ahead of them and several six-packs to comfort them during commercials.

I told him goodbye with what I hoped came off like reluctance, even though I was fairly aggravated with him. I was well aware that earlier he had pulled Lee off to one side and given her the extra set of keys to Max.

"Maggie misplaces things," he'd told her. "This is just in case. Could save you some trouble." True enough, but nobody likes their failings run up a flagpole.

Lee had dropped the keys in her handbag with just a little hint of a smile. She knew it was true that I can't always stay focused on practical stuff; that it goes missing from time to time. Tough, but I also know that most people have some kind of a mental trade-off they have to deal with so I shrug off feelings of incompetence. While folks may call what I have "A.D.D" for "Attention Deficit Disorder." I think of A.D.D. as standing for "Additional Dimension Distinction." Whatever, it's part of who I am.

Dene Hellman

Six

BOTH OF US WERE IN GOOD SPIRITS on that trip. However jumpy Lee may have been about the ordeal coming up, it now seemed to take a back seat to her rising excitement about cruising the four-laner down to Iowa, in Max, on a glorious June day. I was feeling almost equally cheerful. I am a contented person but a few days' break from Jack and the animals and laying out the cards was a nice prospect.

As usual, we laughed at everything. Lee got a special kick out of the conspicuous spectacle that travel-by-convertible presented. It is undeniable that most people ogle convertible drivers and their passengers. It must go back to early Hollywood and the symbols it once set up to designate glamour. The long cigarette holder, as symbol, is long gone. Most people these days have never seen a cocktail shaker in their lives outside of a high priced lounge. That leaves just a few things to identify as glamorous. The convertible is one of them.

I think my own yen to have one dates from a time in my 20s when I was sort of down on my luck in Omaha, hoping I'd pick up a couple of Tarot customers in a bar that would net me enough cash to cover a good meal and a bus ticket back to Madison. As I was headed into the Square Deal, this young blonde driving a blue convertible came oozing down the street. Buckled into the passenger side was a tall green plant, a palm or a corn plant or something, the kind of accessory somebody who lived in a really nice place would choose to decorate their living room. This blonde looked really happy and self-sufficient, chauffeuring that plant as if it was the most delightful thing anybody could do in a day's chores.

That picture was stored someplace in my head, I guess, and had partly fueled my decision to buy Max. Maybe Lee had a convertible image in her head, too, because even though she was always kind and polite to everybody from gas station cashiers to droopy-pants teenagers, when ogling people passed in their tedious sedans she'd sing out, "I'm driving a convertible and you're NOT!"

It was enough to embarrass a drunken sailor, but I swallowed my humility and just laughed along, enjoying her exuberance.

She did throw me off balance when we got near the Iowa border

20

with the Mississippi bridge crossing coming up soon. She pulled the car over into a Wal-Mart lot and got out.

"Maggie," she said, "you are going to drive this car across that bridge. Once you do it, you will lose some of your fears. Make it all the way through Dubuque and I'll pin a medal on you!"

Pleading didn't help and I finally got behind the wheel. When we did the actual crossing I thought of every story about lousy bridge conditions that I'd ever heard or seen on CNN.

"If this structure collapses," I said, "people in a convertible wouldn't have any protection."

"If this structure collapses and we go into the river," said Lee, "we won't have to roll down any windows. We'll be swimming and rescued before anybody else!"

It was no time to question where she got her dubious information and we were over on the Iowa side in no time. From there to Emily's town was an easy two hours and Lee sat back, less giddy now, while I finished the drive.

COUSIN EMILY WAS PLEASED to see us. It had been at least ten years since we'd spent any time with her reviewing our family ties—photo albums and all. We hadn't been out to the cemetery to look at the last decade of tombstones and, since the wedding of Emily's oldest daughter, we hadn't been to a service in the church our great grandparents had helped found. Re-connection was long overdue.

But she'd been warned that on this first evening we were going to change our clothes and be on our way to the reunion in Ratchford before 5:00.

She was reconciled; she understood the importance of events like reunions, probably never missed her own, and was now a little put off by Lee's negative attitude.

"You're just going to have the best time!" she said. "There may be some who don't make it back from other places but hardly anyone who lives around here would think of missing it."

Grumbling under her breath, Lee climbed in and out of the shower, applied some makeup with a light hand, and slipped into her white jeans and clingy green top. Then she pulled her hair into a Miss Proper bun.

"You can't stop me," she said, when I argued for a looser look, but then she compromised a little by letting me pull out some strands of hair here and there to soften the Marion-the-librarian effect.

"Let's go!" she said, but not in the go-to-hell-we're-having-an-adventure-here way that she'd used before. Now there was defiance in her voice. Emily and I exchanged looks as Lee opened the door on Max's driver's side and got behind the wheel.

Seven

LEE HAD TAKEN ON THE AIR of someone determined to drive herself to her own execution. However, as the 12 or so miles from Emily's house to the Ratchford school house decreased, Lee's air of apprehension began to drop away. Actually, every girl who hadn't fit in with the rest of her high school class should have it so good at her later-day reunions. That recognition must have crossed Lee's mind, as well, because by the time we got to the school building her head had an extra tilt. As we parked and got out she gave a little twist that situated her green shirt half a millimeter closer to her impressive breasts.

"This woman is no novice at making an entrance," I thought to myself.

We were on the early side, but 30 or 40 people were already milling around inside the high school gymnasium. Ratchford being a small school, alumni gatherings include every class that ever graduated from there, all at one time. This was the school's 99th anniversary year and some of this year's attendees looked as if they hadn't missed many of the celebrations. Every nursing home for miles around must have been represented.

As people poured in, collected their name tags and joined friends, it was apparent that the middle-aged and older made up the biggest share. Presumably, those younger had better things to do with a Saturday night.

Lee attracted attention from the start. Some knew her. Some didn't. No one knew me until Lee would put her arm around me and identify me as "Maggie, my sister." Then some would say "Oh, yes," because they recalled my parents well and knew they'd had two girls. Obviously, I'd made no more of an impression in school from age five to ten than I had on my Madison teachers in later years. Never, I silently vowed, would anyone catch me at one of these events again.

From the start, I found Lee amazing. Genial, chattering away, laughing, hugging, she bore no resemblance to the scared woman who had driven into Ratchford.

"Who is this charmer?" must have been spread all over my face. Then the answer hit me. This was corporate Lee, Lee of company headquarters mixers, Lee who regularly stood in front of company seminars teaching executives how to write a business letter, how to formulate a speech, how to issue a public relations announcement in front of a television camera.

Lee had come back to her roots having been out in the business and social world, and discovered these good people of Iowa were like everyone else, and that knowing how to work a room was useful everywhere.

Accepting this reunion activity as spectator sport, I became interested in sorting out the varieties of alumni, from local farmers to town folks to out-of-towners, and then the people they had coerced into accompanying them, of which I was an example. One elderly man wearing a guest sticker on his lapel looked as if he was watching Lee with a vested interest similar to mine.

Catching his eye, I ventured a remark. "Are you acquainted with my sister? I'm Maggie Jasper—or was, before I got married."

He beamed and introduced himself. "Earl Door. You might say I'm an acquaintance. I was the Ratchford high school superintendent when she was in school. I always knew this is the way Janilee would be some day! I'm glad to have a chance to see it!"

I took a good look at him. No bad vibes here. The man had no ulterior motives and never had had. He was probably the kind of benign educator the teacher training schools pretend they turn out regularly—patient, kindly, insightful. Also shabby. Unless he and his kind made it into a fairly large school, they were forever doomed to keeping up appearances while stretching every dollar until it lost its give.

Shabbiness among elderly men usually has unintentional reasons. Some of them dress up so seldom that they just keep wearing the same old, same old, never thinking it time to update until the actual time when they have to pull something out of the back of the closet—and then it's too late. Some are long widowed and don't have any daughters to keep track of them. Some are aging bachelors who have turned grumpy and defiant about what they wear. Some might think about going out to get different clothes and just don't have the extra money. Mr. Door didn't look like a person who fit any of those descriptions.

He wasn't a curmudgeon, that's for sure. No grumpy old guy would speak so lovingly of a former student. He looked and spoke like someone who would know the value of being appropriately dressed. While not rolling in money, he'd be the sort who would have a decent tie and shirt in his closet and need them a few times a year. What was with him? He was painfully thin and his fragile skin stretched over his face as if there was nothing underneath except the basic bone structure. I decided he must have been very sick at one time and never had truly recovered.

Polite and gracious as he was, he wasn't about to let me into his head, so I couldn't verify my hunch. The road blocks were up, the same way Lee and Jack put theirs up when they thought I was being too inquisitive. This nice, nice man was hiding a secret. His jacket might smell of mildew and be 20 years out of style; his shirt might be frayed; his tie might be faded beyond any definition of color—but Mr. Door exuded a dignity and poise beyond anyone I'd ever met. I took him by the arm and led him over to Lee.

Lee blinked when I grasped her hand and said, "Mr. Earl Door to see you!" Then she threw her arms around him. This was no forced cordiality. She was really thrilled to see this man.

"Maggie!" she said. "Mr. Door was my inspiration in high school. Every few weeks he'd have a different college catalog to show me. We'd go over them and just read the names of the courses. It was so exciting to think of the things I could study some day and he kept telling me that even though Ratchford wasn't big enough to offer many choices, I'd have it all for the choosing some day and could be anybody I wanted to be!"

"I knew that about you then, Janilee," said Mr. Door, so softly that I had to strain to hear his words. "Please, tell me about your life."

Earl Door and Lee stood there talking. She was excited and filled him in on what she'd done since graduation and what she was doing now. He plied her with questions to encourage her report but I was a little annoyed that she didn't ask him anything about what he'd been doing for the last years.

Worried that he'd notice and be offended, I kept my hand on his arm and one on Lee's arm, for some odd reason thinking my proprietorship would keep them talking until Lee recalled her manners. Frankly, the odor that was emanating from his coat—or person—was a little bit off-putting but, if Lee noticed, it didn't subdue her enthused diary of her accomplishments. It didn't seem to matter to Mr. Door, who eagerly leaned forward to hear all about his one-time favorite.

An older woman stood a few feet away, watching Lee's

performance with a not very pleased expression.

"Probably the wife," I said to myself.

Just then Mr. Door noticed her, too. "Now Janilee," he said, "I know you haven't forgotten Caroline Allan, your home economics teacher!"

The woman came forward, brushing past Mr. Door as if he was invisible. In a split second, Lee was back in corporate charm mode. Affectionately patting Mr. Door on the hand, she turned away from him and laid it on for this Mrs. Caroline Allan thicker than she'd done for all the assembled alumni put together.

"Mrs. Allan!" she purred. "You couldn't guess how often I've thought of you—and with such gratitude! I certainly was never a star pupil of yours but so many things you taught me have come back to my mind over and over again. Would you believe that there was a time when I actually made all my own clothes!"

Mrs. Caroline Allan did her own brand of practiced charm right back at her.

"Why, Janilee," she said. "Better late than never! What made you take up sewing?"

"I was in an office," Lee explained, "and had a chance for a job that required better clothes than I could afford. I just got some woolen yardage and a pattern for a simple, simple dress and went at it as if you were looking over my shoulder! That dress was such a success that I kept on, especially after my late husband, Arthur, found out he just loved shopping for fabrics with me! We'd go into a shop and he'd get so enthused over some fabric that he'd insist I buy it. Before I knew it, I had a stack of patterns and a matching pile of yard goods and always had something cut out or basted up!"

Mrs. Allan nodded as if she, too, understood about always having something cut out or basted up and stuck some kind of thin smile on her face. Nevertheless, it was pretty evident to me that Lee could have whipped up Princess Di's wedding gown and Caroline Allan would have considered it too little, too late.

When the call for dinner was announced, the two women gave each other tight little smiles in a relieved sort of way and parted quickly. All the classes of yore sorted themselves out and headed for their respective areas of the gym. I couldn't see where Mr. Door had gone but guessed there might be a table set aside for former teachers.

As we settled down to our fruit cocktail, ala Del Monte, people continued to straggle in. Lee's classmates were generous with their identifications. "Remember him?" or "Remember her?" was always being asked. Sometimes Lee did and sometimes she didn't, but she was always grateful for the assistance.

Eight

A MAN WHO LOOKED TO BE about Lee's age entered alone, picked up his name tag and when our table was pointed out he started toward us, stopping every now and again to shake hands with someone encountered along the way.

"Remember Ben Deckard?" asked the nice farmer sitting across from us.

Lee's spoon paused on its way to a diced pear. Then she recovered and said, "Sure do. Graduated a couple of years before us, didn't he?"

She leaned over to me and whispered, "Only person in high school smarter than me!"

This Ben Deckard didn't have the advantage of receiving prior identification as to who we were, but Lee's fellow alum corrected that by calling out as he approached, "Look who's here! Janilee Jasper!"

I could have sworn I saw fireworks exploding over the guy's head. Maybe I really did. He reached out to shake Lee's hand. She did the same. It was one of those first-time meetings when my psychic powers tell me a couple might just as well cut to the chase and jump into bed.

Lee smiled then, eyes wide, and said, "This is my sister, Maggie Presnall."

Ben sat down in the empty chair on my other side and Lee turned back to the table with a look on her face that confirmed she had just caught a preview glimpse of paradise.

"Something just happened here," I said to myself. "Lee never mentioned any Ben Deckard in our recent memory lane chats. This must have been an old flame she didn't want to talk about."

Lee leaned across me once and said to Ben, "What are you reading?"

"What are you reading?" my head screamed. *"What happened to questions like, 'Are you still farming?' 'Do you have a family living in Ratchford?' 'How is your mother?'"*

Ben didn't seem to find the question odd. "Mostly agriculture journals, any more," he replied.

Lee went back to conversation with former classmates and Ben started politely poking questions at me.

"Is Janilee's husband here?"

"Where do you and Janilee live?"

"Are you and Janilee teachers?"

"Dead." "Down South." "Communication specialists." were my replies at the appropriate moments.

I sized Ben up between questions. He was tall and farmer-muscular, with wavy medium-brown hair and piercing blue eyes that took in a lot more than he let on he was seeing. At one time I maybe could have gone for him myself but I could see he was much closer to being attracted to someone really brainy and educated like Lee. He told me that he farmed north of town and I usually am comfortable with farmers, but this guy projected something out of the usual. At the moment, however, all I could see in his head, was "Janilee, Janilee, Janilee." Since they'd evidently known one another long ago, it couldn't exactly qualify as love at first sight this evening but it certainly seemed to carry some of the same stunned quality.

Always the observer, I decided this was a live and learn situation for me. At the end of the dinner and way too many remarks later by the people in charge of the alumni program, it was no particular surprise when Ben leaned across me and said to Lee, "Will you and Maggie come out to my farm this evening so we'll have a chance to catch up?"

Even though they'd exchanged no more than three remarks during the dinner, it didn't surprise me that Lee said, "How nice of you, Ben! We would love to!"

I could feel the sisterly pinch, even though mentally applied, and brightly and dutifully said, "Why sure! The night is young!"

29

Nine

AND THE NIGHT *WAS* YOUNG as we stepped out into it. In mid-summer in the upper Midwest, dark doesn't fall until after 9:30 and we had well over an hour to go. The three of us, Lee, Ben and I, walked out into it, Lee with such a dazed look on her face that she didn't even say goodbye to the people she had just been reunited with.

I saw Mr. Door, her old superintendent, standing off to one side and dropped back to say a few words to him. He was watching Ben and Lee and when he looked at me I nodded toward them and shrugged.

He laughed. "That's good! That's good! Do you know how many times I tried to push them together when they were in high school? One year I even jiggered the seating in study hall so their desks would be diagonally across from one another!"

Cackling like a yenta who has seen her best matchmaking skills come to fruition, Earl Door loped off into the Ratchford evening. It felt to me as if he had simply been there that night to make one last effort to bring two former favorites of his into sighting range of each other.

Dismissing the thought, I caught up with Lee and Ben and found them leaning on Max, talking. He was giving her directions to his farm.

"Five miles out," he said, "to County Road D. You can follow me. There's a tricky turnoff that goes a couple of miles down. If you're not looking for it, you might miss it."

Ben's pickup was parked down the street a little way and we waited until he pulled out. Lee was still driving us, to my relief. I waited until we hit the edge of town, which took about three minutes, and on the gravel surface of the first road.

"What in hell," I just about shouted, "makes you willing to head into a strange place with somebody you haven't laid eyes on in thirty years? There must've been someplace in town where we could have gotten coffee and sat in a booth like civilized folks, and caught up on your past histories!"

Lee smiled and tapped Max's dashboard affectionately. "Maximum Freedom," she said, "is a bad influence!"

By now we were well down the road and the gravel dust was kicking up clouds that were enough to choke a herd of wildebeests. The convertible top was still down and what was happening to Max's black leather upholstery was something I didn't want to think about. I just stared at Lee, waiting for a better explanation.

"Can't quite figure it out either," she admitted. "Ben and I never dated. We were both too shy to even talk much. His last year in high school, he asked me to dance at the alumni reunion. They used to end them with a dance back then, and that was open to everybody, even kids still in high school. Ben had just graduated and I had just finished tenth grade. We danced all evening and at first we didn't talk because we didn't know what to say, and then we didn't talk because it felt as if we were so much a part of each other that we didn't need to. Then the dance was over and he didn't even ask if I'd like a ride home. I was kind of sad about that, but then managed to put him out of my mind. All these years, I don't think I've thought about him more than once every five years."

She was quiet for a moment or two. Then she added, "When he walked in tonight it was as if no time had gone by and I was still standing there on the edge of the dance floor after the music stopped, wondering if he wasn't going to ask if he could take me home."

"Oh," I said. There didn't seem to be any more to ask or say. Just, "Oh."

By now, we were off the gravel and driving down a narrow side road that made the first road look like the Eisenhower Expressway. This back road passed some pretty farms, spaced a good distance apart. Lee spied a name on one of the mailboxes.

"That's the Allan's place," she said. "I forgot that they were neighbors to the Deckards."

"Who?" I asked, then remembered meeting Lee's former home economics teacher, Caroline Allan of the sour face.

We bumped over a one-lane bridge that looked as if it had seen better days. A mile or so farther, Ben's pickup turned into a grassy farmyard.

"Nice night," he said, walking over to meet us as we got out of the car. "I wish it would be light longer so I could show you around the farm, but maybe another time. Come on in and I'll brew us some coffee!"

Lee still had a semi-dazed look on her face. If Ben had offered a barefoot tour of the hog house right then and there, she would have

31

followed him, no questions asked. I, however, took my time looking over our surroundings. This farm was a long way from anyplace else, which made me kind of uneasy, and some of the vibes I was picking up were on the eerie side.

It was fairly obvious from the lack of frills that a man lived here alone. The barn and other visible outbuildings, and the cattle pen fenced in close by, looked well kept up, painted where paint was required and immaculately neat overall. No rusty machinery scattered around, no unhoused equipment of any kind. The grass had been recently mowed close to the ground in wide tractor-width swaths that didn't conceal a ground-cover mixture of bluegrass, broad-leaf weeds and dandelion stubble. The house was something else again. Dingy and unpainted, it looked as if it might fall in on itself any day. Compared with the farm operation, evidently nobody had cared about it in a long time. There had probably once been a yard, therefore the bluegrass remnants, but it was hard to make out where it began and ended. A row of peony bushes, probably as old as the house, were shedding this year's bloom and predictably were going to be swallowed by overgrown vegetation before the summer was over. An old timey two-seated wooden glider stood off to the side. I recalled the one that had stood in my grandparents' yard when I was a little girl and a little twinge of homesickness or nostalgia or some such feeling nudged me.

Lee and Ben were on the front porch which, incidentally, looked about ready to separate into pieces—a cement riser here, a crumbling step there, a sagging wooden pillar about to collapse. Ben was unlocking the front door.

"I always use the back door," he said, "but you're company so you're getting the full benefit of my wonderful housekeeping."

That the wonderful housekeeping would have had to be done at least 20 years ago, was pretty evident as we walked into a standard farmhouse living room, circa 1950, that smelled as if no one had opened a window since Sputnik went into space. I'm not given to running a white-gloved finger over furnishings, my own or anybody else's, but as we followed Ben through the room, I tried not to brush against anything.

We made it through a similarly moldy-looking dining room, back into a big kitchen that was probably where Ben spent his indoor hours. From the cracked harvest gold, avocado green linoleum to the Formica table and chairs, I surmised this room had been pretty current sometime mid-twentieth century.

Ben looked at Lee with a grimace of apology, as if he hadn't realized until just this minute how the farmhouse would appear to a new visitor.

"Well, I keep this room semi-clean," he laughed. "You're going to have to cut me some slack. I've lived here alone for quite a few years."

Lee murmured something reassuring and Ben set about measuring out some coffee and water. At least his coffeepot was an up-to-date drip model. I planned to reserve judgment until I got a look at the cups he'd use to serve us.

"Would you like to see the rest of the house?" he asked. "If we get it over with, we can pretend it isn't there for the rest of the evening!"

"Yes," Lee said. "It's really very charming. I never knew your mother, but she must have been a very interesting lady."

"About as charming as a chicken coop," I said to myself. "If there's anything here that suggests his mother might have been interesting, I've missed it."

I kept quiet, though, assuming Lee meant well and Ben would be pleased at the thought of having interesting parentage.

"Yes and no," Ben said to Lee. "She and Dad both had a couple of years of college before they started farming the old family homestead, and she had once liked to play the piano. But keeping up a farm is hard work. She helped my dad, and then my brother came along and then I was born three years later and after that she always had her hands full with cooking and the vegetable garden, and her chickens and doing a little something at the church."

We climbed narrow stairs. Ben opened the first door. "My room," he said, closing it quickly but not before we glimpsed an interior with a single-width unmade bed and a dresser piled high with an assortment of roughly folded work clothes.

Another, bigger, bedroom looked as if it had been moved out of, then tidied up into a permanent state of respectability that no later neglect could diminish.

"The folks' room," Ben said. "Mother moved into town to live with her sister shortly after Karl died. Dad had passed on before and she just didn't seem to have any more enthusiasm for staying on the farm."

Another door, another room. "Karl's," Ben said. He opened the door a crack, as if he was fearful we might actually look.

"I didn't know Karl was gone," said Lee. "I didn't know him personally since he was ahead of us in school, but I knew him when I saw him in town. May I ask what happened?"

"Freak farm accident," Ben said, shutting the door abruptly but not in time to avoid an ugly essence of some kind from whipping out to personally smack me in the face. However, I am a pro and didn't change expression.

"Let's go see if the coffee is done!" said Ben and Lee and I obediently followed him downstairs. I went last and caught myself looking back over my shoulder to see if we were being trailed by anything sinister. It was hard for me to deny that something was standing guard in the upstairs hall.

Ben set out big white coffee mugs. About what I expected, I thought, looking into the bottom of mine before he filled it. Stains that could have used a bath in Clorox solution testified to too many years of cold water rinses. "Where am I getting this fastidious attitude?" I asked myself. Maybe I was being watchful for Lee. Clearly, from everything I saw, Ben didn't make a practice of entertaining lady friends and I relaxed my vigilance.

The three of us sat around the table, cradling our cups. Ben politely asked to be told how Lee and I spend our time and where. We, polite in return, asked the same of him. I knew I was going to have to figure out a way to leave them alone and managed a quick synopsis.

"Married to a carpenter. Live in a small town in Wisconsin. Do counseling work," summed my life up efficiently.

Lee was next and, in effect, said, "Went to the University of Missouri. Widow. Two grown sons. Work as kind of an English teacher in a big corporation in the South."

Ben was brief, too. "Went to college in Ames. Uncle Sam got me. Went back to college afterward. Came back to the farm to help after Dad got sick. Stayed."

It was time for my exit. "It's such a beautiful evening," I said. "The old swing out in the yard really calls to me because our grandparents had one like it. If you don't mind, I think I'll go and try it out."

Ben and Lee got to their feet as soon as I did and walked me through the front rooms. As I meandered to where the wooden glider stood, between the house and the road, they lingered on the porch.

From my seat on the glider I could see them across the yard, deep in conversation, Ben perched on one of the cement risers that framed the steps, Lee leaning against one of the crumbling pillars.

If I watched them, I thought, I'd just be trying to figure what was going on between them and how long it would be before Lee and I could take off for Emily's house. Besides, it was the kind of soft summer night that invited me to merge with it.

Night noises called. Off in the distance farm animals were making low comments about the state of affairs on the Deckard farm. The glider, not used to having company, creaked in what seemed, at first, like complaints but later became companionable answering responses to my thoughts. These turned into voices that spoke of former times.

How long the swing had been there, I couldn't say, but judging from what I knew about the one that had stood on my grandparent's farm, I'd guess these structures had been popular Sears and Roebuck offerings in the 1920s. There had to have been a time, maybe up through the time Ben's parents ran the farm, when this particular one had been kept in repair and painted once in a while. Now, as I sat in it, it began to tell me about times when it was used to rock farm babies to sleep and entertain toddlers. It spoke of other times when it swayed under the weight of courting lovers, and still others when harried young husbands and wives came out in the cool of the evening for an hour or two away from the demands of young children and never-ending farm work.

Across the fields—old fields that were first planted before the Civil War—along a creek that ran through an aged grove of trees, I could now hear a quiet shuffle of feet, the feet of the Indians who long ago had passed through on their way to campgrounds along the Skunk River. Was this where I was getting the sense of uneasiness that had begun in the upstairs hall? So much history was alive and breathing all around me.

I was startled when Lee suddenly appeared beside the swing. "Want to go?" she asked. "Sorry to have kept you waiting."

"It was fine," I said, perfectly aware that she would no way, at the moment, be receptive to an explanation of how I'd been passing the time in communication with prior generations.

Ben walked us out and helped put the top up on Max. "See you," he said as he and Lee touched hands. He lifted his hand in a mock salute as we drove out of the farmyard.

Lee had almost nothing to say on our way back to Emily's house and, tired, I didn't push. It was almost midnight when we got there, even later when we finally got to bed in the guest room. I woke up at 8:00 the next morning, late for me. As soon as my eyes focused, they lit on a note on Lee's pillow. "Went back to the farm," it said. "See you tonight."

There was no Max in Emily's driveway. Lee had put her extra set of car keys to use and was gone.

Book Two: Lee

Ten

SUMMER MORNINGS IN IOWA begin early and clear. Having grown accustomed to the slow-to-rise dawning of a Carolina day, this pungent start seemed right. Last night Ben had asked if I'd consider coming back to the farm. Without a decent pause to consider, I'd said yes.

To appropriate Max and leave Maggie without explanation or discussion was obnoxious behavior in my code. How could I ever excuse it?

By saying, "I'm sorry, but I think I just met the love of my life and I have to go find out right away?"

Or, "I just dropped off the edge of the world at this Ratchford school reunion and it has become necessary to test reality?"

Maggie wouldn't have bought it, of course. Having elected freedom of thought and deed for herself from the time she hit puberty, she then discovered that her own comfort lay in a reasoned view of the world. Bottom line: I live by a strenuous set of self-imposed expectations and am ever in search of the ideal. Only through continual internal dialogue and the settling of age have I contained my demons of simmering lust and a tendency to perfectionism. Or so I tell myself.

Maggie lives free of self-criticism and is a pragmatist, believing:

People get what they ask for.

Kindness is good; common sense is better.

There are no true loves or soul mates; just people you prefer to have in your life.

It is essential, at all times, to understand the rules of self-protection.

This is the gospel she preaches to those who seek answers by way of her psychic gifts. Generally, they are fortunate that it is. It saves those who heed her words a lot of untidy misery and it keeps them coming back for more.

That I march to a different drummer is a basis for ongoing sisterly discussion. We think it is probably a result of being a Ratchford misfit. A combination of painful shyness, a volcanic imagination, and being dressed like a princess by a well-meaning mother almost guaranteed me the scorn of rural classmates.

Accustomed to having both my vocabulary and my appearance ridiculed, I resorted more and more to books where the characters thought and talked like me. Since these were often inhabitants of 18th or 19th century England, I was rendered even less fit for conversation in a 20th century farm community.

"Please, Sir," I would say to a gawky math teacher who was a mere two years out of teachers' college and much preferred his duties as a basketball coach, "May I test my abilities with these equations before planning next semester's challenges?"

"Huh?" he would say, backing off as far as decency permitted.

Fortunately, the mirror gave me back a tolerable image whenever I was despondent about being a wallflower. While I admired LaVerne Schmidt's blonde hair and blue eyes, it wasn't because I felt physically inadequate in comparison. I was perfectly content to have darker hair and skin than others in that Northern European heritage pod—rather pleased, in fact, to be different. Believing that Cinderella grew up to capture the prince, I was confident that my fate would mimic hers.

Now, I smile ruefully. In truth, there had been a scarcity of princes in grownup life and none that accrued to me. Arthur, a dear man who was both pleasant and remote, would have puzzled over what to do with a glass slipper but he provided my children with some decent genes. As Cinderella, I would have had to be the one to pick the slipper up from the ballroom floor, devise a method for him to find me, and show him how to try it on my foot to assure fit.

WHEN I LEFT RATCHFORD for college at age 17, there were two sides to my personality. On the one hand, I felt equal to any kind of work that might be called for in my studies and I was also confident that getting away from home and making my own decisions would cure some of my problems with finding friends.

It was amazing how well things fell into place. I was euphoric about getting away from Ratchford but, among other freshman girls, some of whom were scared at being away from home for the first time in their lives. I evidently came across as reasonable friend material. With a chance to start over, minus the "stuck up" label assigned to me by the Ratchford kids, I was more than ready to socialize. The reward was companionship with some outstanding women who would come into their own by their last college years. Some of them are still in my life.

One side of me that I kept hidden was my almost total naivety about guys. Being a wallflower in high school, sans brothers and with a kind father who, nonetheless, always seemed to be at his job and overworked until the day he just up and dropped dead, I knew nothing about the thoughts and behavior of the other sex. In my first two years of college, I nearly always accepted immediately if a guy asked me for a date, thrilled to be a belle at last. If, as often happened, my date expected far more sexual activity than I found comfortable, I was likely to reject him with a vehemence that he found astonishing. That left me in a state of cringing embarrassment when next we ran into one another on campus.

My ongoing conversation with myself was:

Q. "What are those other girls—the ones who date all the time—doing?"

A. "They must be so much more fun than I am!" or "They know how to make guys respect them!"

Hah!

Arthur was different and a blessed relief. When we occupied adjoining seats in a third-year business leadership class, he shyly asked me out and followed up with pricey dates that impressed my girlfriends. When I got back to the dorm after an evening with him, they would oh and ah.

"He *really* took you to Chantilly Gardens for dinner?" they would marvel, and I would nod with the tiniest bit of complacency.

Arthur and I dated for two months before he asked for a kiss and then waited another two before sticking his tongue into my mouth. By the end of the school year I was raging with lust but Arthur kept me pure. I'd go at him with the enthusiasm of a young circus lion salivating over its inept trainer and he'd chidingly hold me at arm's length.

"Let's keep the roses, for now, and postpone the dynamite," he'd say.

Arthur, of course, was following the script his successful executive father had laid down. "Don't get anybody pregnant. Find a nice girl we can all be proud of. Marry her and bring her home to Charlotte. I'll take care of the rest."

Interesting, isn't it, how many of us live out the scripts a parent has written for us? We may not even realize it until years later—because the details have been changed—but there we are, being and doing what a parent essentially wanted. Arthur and I had that in common.

Eleven

BY CHRISTMAS OF OUR SENIOR YEAR, I was sporting a diamond engagement ring that wowed everybody we knew, especially my approving mother who could happily see her dreams for me were coming true. She regretted not giving me a big church sendoff in Ratchford or Madison after I graduated, but listened graciously when Arthur's father explained that our wedding was an important local social occasion that would bode well for Arthur's business future. She was pretty happy about playing mother of the bride in Charlotte and made elaborate plans, with the help of a Charlotte wedding planner, while Arthur's widower father, Milton, picked up all the bills for a country club event that made the *Charlotte Observer* purr.

As a wedding gift, Milton gave us the big, lovely colonial-style house in the gated community where he and his late wife had raised Arthur. Convinced that he had done right by us and could now go play for a while, maybe for the first time in his life, he then moved into a posh new condo in Dilworth that made him feel –and act—like a sophisticated stud. After naming Arthur a junior partner in his insurance brokerage firm, he walked away and spent his next three years squiring gorgeous women to various worldwide destinations. Arthur did his best to pretend competence while Milton's right-hand man of many years, Paul Davis, actually called the shots in the office.

Our house was pleasant but, since I'd had little to do with choosing it and it came furnished, I subsided into housewifery with ambivalent feelings. There was something nice about our living in a *Southern Living* setting but I kept asking myself if this was all there was going to be and did I dare change the wall color in the dining room?

Every day I fixed breakfast while Arthur got ready to go to the office. After he left I took a shower, put on makeup, and did rudimentary housekeeping. No need to sweat it, Milton arranged for his former maid to come in twice a week to do the hard stuff.

I wandered around the garden and wondered what might be done to make it more original and captivating. Again, no need to sweat it; Milton's former gardener came often to do the tough stuff and he didn't seem to want any suggestions from me. Cowed, I didn't make any.

I tried cooking but knew absolutely nothing about it and settled for basic recipes from Mother's Ratchford Congregational Church cookbook. It didn't matter because Arthur was a delicate eater who folded up his napkin beside his plate about the time I was ready for a second helping.

As a husband, Arthur turned out to be a lukewarm lover but a very kind man who never complained about anything. I was ashamed of the lack of enthusiasm for him that I developed within months and flagellated myself mercilessly, mentally comparing my indifference to the cruelty of historic villainesses.

"He is so good," I told myself, "and he works so hard to be a provider and a good son to his father. He must never find out how unloving and ungrateful I really feel."

Twelve

WITHIN 14 MONTHS WE WERE PARENTS to a wonderful baby boy, and less than two years later we had a matched set. Joe and Tim provided the answer to much of the lack I felt in my life, gave me more than enough to do, and gave Arthur a nice glow of accomplishment, as well.

Milton was, by this time, making an ass of himself over a secretary he had met in a European consulate. Arthur was pushed into trying to keep the business together, feebly but the best he knew how, and didn't want to distress his father by owning up to problems with getting and keeping customers, not being respected by the office staff, and being subtly ridiculed by Paul Davis.

DISGUSTED AT THE WHOLE SCENARIO and looking out for himself, Davis decided to leave the firm and start his own insurance business. A long-time associate of Milton's, he knew most of the customers and his conviviality must have compared favorably, in their eyes, to Arthur's meekness. Milton may have been the glue that once held the business together but Paul Davis had learned a lot, over the years, about running an insurance brokerage. One Friday afternoon in July, he broke the news about leaving and was a no-show the following Monday morning.

After Paul moved on, Arthur was left with only the not-so-successful clients and no idea how to woo new and more lucrative ones. He drastically cut his own salary and we dismissed the maid and garden help. If we hadn't been given our house, free and clear, we would have lost it. For the sake of the boys, I begged him not to mortgage it to meet the shortfall and went looking for work myself. A double major in English and Speech was not a perfect vehicle for landing a job that paid well so it took me awhile to find something suitable.

Milton, who thought he had generously provided for Arthur and family, as well as for his own belated youth, went on indulging himself beyond the limits of good sense. He may have lost a lot of money but wasn't about to lose his new lifestyle and girlfriend and spent down almost everything he had accumulated over the years. Arthur timidly suggested he come home for a while and try to get the business in shape but one night Milton toppled, drunk, off a pier and into the Mediterranean and that was it. He came home, all right, but only to be interred next to Arthur's mother in the family's cemetery-of-choice.

As the business dwindled, Arthur dwindled with it. It turned out that there was good reason for his lack of energy. He had developed a serious blood disease that robbed him of vitality. Before long, the business truly went kaput and, sadly, he came home to live the life of an invalid.

On the good side, I finally found a decent job that held the promise of advancement. Arthur's family had been well connected so I got a couple of interviews with local mover and shaker types. Thus, I ended up in a narrow cubicle where I helped transform bank documents into approximate English. This was identified as "technical writing." It was more boring than Mother's Congregational ladies' cookbook but with zilch social life and no mortgage payments, we could now meet the taxes and raise the boys.

Arthur became more and more like a semi-visible ghost. He stood up to his failing health with courage and soft-spoken resignation and I admired him. He may not have turned out to be a Prince Charming but he was a good man. Thanks to decent medical insurance offered through my job, we could meet most of his needs up to and including the time his leukemia killed him. The rest of our medical debt was something I'd have to cope with for years to come.

Milton had set up education trusts for the boys when they were born, which was before his money ran out, so they comfortably made it through school, including prestigious universities and advanced degrees. I suppose I wrote their scripts for them, just as my mother and Arthur's father had done for us. Not as hung up on money and comfort as our parents were, I preached saving the world to my kids, naming conservation, poverty and worldwide education as good places to start.

By the time of this, my latest trip to visit Maggie, I was single and had a good job that included travel. I still lived in the nice house that Milton had given Arthur and me but a 20 year fast-forward found me a gourmet cook and an ardent horticulturist. I missed my boys but was proud that they were off in the world doing worthwhile things. Joe was on the other side of the world working with Greenpeace and Tim was involved in an important archeology dig someplace in South America. When I could, I worked with a group that rescued endangered plants but how much time can you spend communicating with ladyslippers and ferns? About once a year, my Missouri U. girlfriends and I spent a few days catching up on each other's lives. Mostly, we met at my place in Charlotte because it had plenty of room for visitors and lots of privacy for telling funny and indelicate tales about our lives. I loved cooking for our get-togethers and proudly sent my friends home with plant starts from my garden.

FROM TIME TO TIME there were men in my life; my job almost guaranteed a lot of variety. I had eventually been named as the company's communication specialist and travelled to branch offices across the country. While I stood in various conference centers explaining how to handle a hostile television interviewer or warning about the pitfalls of a business buffet that included dripping shrimp cocktail sauce, I would be sized up by various levels of executives and one or more of them was likely to hit on me later in the day.

No problem. Tactfully and sweetly, as befits a Southern lady, I could get rid of the ones who did not appeal and the ones who were married. Once in a while, some one of the men interested me and I would tentatively explore the possibility of a relationship. It was the rare individual who lasted longer than six months before I dismissed him, also tactfully and sweetly. I tried not to leave a trail of broken hearts, mine included, but inevitably wondered afterward what it was that I was looking for. Ideally, it would be someone with more on his mind than climbing the corporate ladder or improving his golf score.

"I'll know him if I see him," I promised Maggie whenever she got on my case. That was a good deal more pulp-fiction sentiment than I appreciated in myself, but I went on looking.

Life was reasonably satisfactory but I was lonely.

Thirteen

THIS BEN WHO HAD CAUSED my early Sunday morning flight from Cousin Emily's house was an exciting enigma. On the one hand, I didn't know him at all, but on the other hand I had known him since my girlhood. This must be the charm of postponed reunions, I thought. You return to your youth, meet appealing strangers, but don't have to spend time finding out about their roots. You were there at the creation. You know about their families, how smart they are, and their essential mode of conduct. Beginning with that knowledge, the decision to explore farther or not is an easy one to make.

In the case of Ben, I knew he came from a reputable farm family, that he had always been into books, much as I had, that he was infinitely intelligent, that he was inclined to avoid the limelight but was stubborn about following his own interests. Few farm boys are the valedictorians of their class but Ben had been, thanks to relentless, self-imposed study. I also knew there was unfinished business between us. It had been dormant for more than 30 years and, now that I had a current look at him, it was time to see if it should be awakened.

Last night had yielded clues. As we talked outside on the front porch, rapidly covering the basics of where we'd been and who we now were, we were both obviously putting a best foot forward and looking to set it on common ground. This was territory that would have to be revisited in detail if our acquaintance continued. For now, there was an uncanny sense that in our separate places and separate ways we had arrived at a mutual destination.

When Ben excused himself for what I assumed was a bathroom break, I followed him into the kitchen to check for leftover coffee. After he left the room, I glanced at the clutter at one end of the big table. The agricultural journals he had referred to earlier were casually scattered and a book spine was partially uncovered.

While I would never open anyone's mail or dresser drawers unbidden, I am—I admit it—a voyeur of the books people read. Lifting an agriculture magazine, I read the title of the book under it and lost my heart. It was Whitman's *Leaves of Grass.* Its presence there on the kitchen table among the reading materials of everyday life told me Ben had the kind of thoughts I cherished. Maggie may scoff but, for me, the sexiest quality a man can have is high intelligence tempered by sensitivity.

When Ben asked me if I'd come back the next day, I had already made up my mind that I would.

THE NEXT MORNING he came bounding over to the car as soon as I drove in. He had been waiting eagerly, it seemed.

"I'll take that farm tour now," I said, sliding off Max's front seat in what I hoped was a graceful display of legs. "Thank God for those gut-wrenching workouts at the gym," I reflected.

This Ben was a man in love with his land and his work. That was obvious as I followed him around the farm. His primary cash flow, he said, derived from a good-sized herd of beef cattle and many of his cultivated crops had to do with feeding and pasturing them. Thanks to a vast accumulation of acres, over the years, he also grew the usual cash crops. He had told me that last evening, emphasizing that his cattle were not pumped full of chemicals or fed dubious supplements.

The only times I had previously looked at large bunches of cows were during movies where they were obligatory accessories, bellowing, stampeding, moving along toward Dodge. In comparison, these seemed to lead placid lives, chewing thoughtfully and standing around a lot. I couldn't think of any intelligent questions to ask, even though I searched my brain for enough material to formulate a reasonable query. "What are they reading?" certainly wouldn't do.

We drifted into a big barn where Ben pointed out the physical equipment related to breeding and raising cattle and administering to the animals' occasional veterinarian needs. A man who looked older than Ben climbed down from the hay mow, saw us, blushed, and tried to back off.

"Janilee, this is Ernest Weist," Ben said. "Ernest helps me with the farm work."

Ernest nodded and ducked speedily out of the barn. Ben laughed. "I guess he wasn't expected to see a woman," he said. "There haven't been any of those around for a long time. Right now, you might as well be an alien from another planet. I'll tell him later that you used to be a Ratchford town girl. It could be that he knew your folks."

"Does he live nearby?" I asked, grateful for the distraction from the cows.

"Comes out from town," Ben said. "He grew up on a farm west of Main Street but he had some rotten luck in the '80s and had to sell out. We all felt bad when everything on his farm was auctioned off, but it happens. Seemed as if all Ernest knew how to do or cared to do was farm. He used to hire out wherever he could find work. Then quite a while back I took him on full time. Maybe I should rephrase and say that he and I took one another on. Anyway, he's good, responsible help and he covers for me when I need to be in Des Moines or someplace on business."

I quirked an eyebrow, thinking my inner picture of Ben didn't include images of him anywhere but in Ratchford territory. Nor was he away a lot, he explained, but he was on some agriculture and conservation committees on a state level. "It keeps me a social creature," he laughed. "I don't want to get so farm-bound that I lose touch with the rest of the world!"

Good news in a way, I thought, trying to look at him objectively. I preferred men with wide interests, but now a finger's worth of jealousy stirred my gut. Just who did he socialize with? Did he have women friends or, worse, a particular woman friend? Was I faced with competition and what did a Carolina widow whose chief expertise lay in the niceties of corporate communications have to offer an attractive, prosperous Iowa farmer?

Our tour continued. Contrary to memories of my grandparents' farm, there were no pigs or chickens. "Mother's folks," I ventured, "had one of those farms that were homesteaded in the 1800s and passed down, generation after generation. Then there wasn't another generation that wanted to farm and it was sold."

"This one has been in the family since prairie days," said Ben. "Only we were lucky that every generation wanted to keep it going and add to it. There's an old orchard and I can show you where the smokehouse and springhouse were. The house is almost that old. It got rebuilt about every 40 years but the core is still there. And it sure can use another makeover!

"There's an old, old grove of trees over there," he added. "It has a creek running through it where Karl and I used to fish for bullheads. Sometimes we'd splash around in it but it took a very rainy year to make it deep enough for swimming. We used to find arrowheads, so we knew people had been there since before history books."

"Show me," I said.

Fourteen

WE HIKED OVER ROUGH PASTURE TO THE TREELINE, climbing through barbed wire fence strands that Ben courteously held up for me.

"I'm surprised it's still here," I said, charmed by the little grove.

"It's probably the only stand of virgin timber for many, many miles," said Ben. "It has always seemed too special to destroy, I guess. Every spring the bluebells and Dutchmen's britches come up thick. As long as Mother was able, she liked to hike over here in May and gather a bouquet."

"It's heaven on earth," I thought, remembering those visits to my grandparents' farm when I was a little girl. As long as the bull was in a closed-off area, nobody cared where I went. When I got tired of cuddling the kittens that had been born in the barn, or sitting in the goose pen adoring the goslings, I'd wander off to a pasture, pretending to gallop with a phantom band of Indians. In the winter I'd climb snow drifts, envisioning the marble halls and circular staircases of the storybooks I'd been reading since I was eight. The stand of trees that offered shade to roving cows in hot summers marked off boundaries, from trunk to trunk, for my imaginary houses. And on each tree I had located a secret door that I pretended might open to reveal fairy occupants.

I sat down on a fallen log. "You must never, never let anything happen to destroy this!" I said with a passion that then made me feel a little foolish.

Ben did not laugh. "Not as long as I live!" he vowed.

It was a good place to linger and talk. Ben told me he had asked Ernest to take over the essential chores for both of them today.

"When you were in high school," I asked, "did you plan to be a farmer?"

"Not exactly," was the reply. "That was more the idea Karl had, so there wasn't any concern about who would help out at home. Mr. Door put me on to some books that opened some other ideas. By the way, do you remember him?"

"I talked to him at the reunion last night" I answered. "Didn't you?"

Ben frowned slightly. "Didn't see him. Wish I had. It's been

49

quite a few years since he came back to Ratchford and he seemed really old at that time. I'm surprised he's still alive.

"But I did come in late. And after that, I just saw you," he added, with a shy smile.

"Anyway," I said, "what were the books he suggested?"

"*Silent Spring*, for one. It had been out for a few years when I first read it and had created quite a stir, with its warnings about the pesticides and the chemicals being put in the ground. Didn't go over real well in Iowa. Even now, there are farmers who try to deny a lot of what it said."

"And the other books?" I asked.

"Well," he said, "there was this professor up in Wisconsin at the University who was talking conservation in ways that we hadn't thought about. Last name was Leopold. Book called *Sand County Almanac*. It had been around for a while but it still was an eye-opener.

"I decided what I wanted to do was get into conservation some way and do something that needed doing for the world."

THIS WAS DEFINITELY MY KIND OF MAN. "So how have you followed through?" I asked, my eagerness overshadowing my manners.

Ben grew visibly uncomfortable, shifting his weight around on the log and looking off through the trees as if he was trying to remember some previously rehearsed lines.

"Tried," he said. "Got a pretty good start on preparing for a conservation career, with some time off that Uncle Sam insisted on. Even got married after I got out of the Army and had finished a fair amount of graduate school."

This was information of the first degree. "Married?" I said, in a tone that I hoped wasn't shrill.

Ben seemed easy about answering that one. "Couple of years. Turned out it wasn't a marriage made in heaven and when the folks really needed me on the farm she said she didn't have any intention of being a farmer's wife. So that was that."

"Was that at the time of Karl's death?" I asked.

Ben looked at me a few seconds before answering. It had, I realized, been a long time since he'd felt he had to explain his family's business to anyone. In small rural communities people figure out pretty soon how it goes for others. There is very little heart-to-heart talk and a great deal of minding of one's own business. While rumors fly and gossip thrives, personal interaction relies heavily on saving face for one another.

"No," he said. "Karl didn't die then. He just wasn't in good health."

He looked off into space a few seconds more, then added, "Truth is, he wasn't real stable, mentally. Couldn't get out of bed, some days, and our father was going through the kidney failure that ended up killing him. Just wasn't much choice for me except to come home and take over."

"From the other things you've told me," I said, "I'd guess that these days you're using your interests and education to work in state policy organizations as well as on your own farm."

Ben's expression cleared. It wasn't something he spelled out to people but his face said he was glad that I realized it.

"Come on," he said, pulling me up off the log. "I don't keep fancy groceries in the house and we can go to town and have Sunday dinner or we can open a can of tuna."

Looking down at my khaki shorts, it wasn't a hard decision.

"I didn't come dressed for Sunday dinner in Ratchford," I said. "Let's go back to the house and see what you have in cans."

Fifteen

"SWEET" ISN'T A WORD I like very much. I had never in my life wanted to be described as "sweet," since for years I unfairly equated it with a certain amount of mental vacancy or, at the least, diminished personality. The emotions I had felt while rocking and caring for my two infant sons went way beyond "sweet." These days, with Tim and Joe so far away, some of my favorite daydreams were about someday having grandchildren. That would be as "sweet" as I could envision.

But the afternoon Ben and I shared was one of the sweetest I had ever experienced. There wasn't a topic introduced into conversation that wasn't excitingly ripe for mutual ideas. The wonder lay in finding someone who even thought about the same things I did. Differences in opinion were mere sparks that ignited the wish to go on talking as long as possible.

He talked about repositories for seed varieties that could otherwise be lost to the world of agriculture.

I talked about moving endangered wild flowers to sheltered environments where they could avoid being poached.

He talked about the problems involved with getting farmers to back off from dosing their animals with hormones.

I talked about my boys' involvement with Greenpeace and the preservation of artifacts that could so easily be stolen and sold.

While Ben put together a bit of lunch, I looked into the niche off the kitchen where he did bookwork, listened to music and read. He claimed that he mostly read farming magazines but, kneeling on a less than pristine floor, I investigated a pile of current books that ranged from history to physiology. Some I had read, others had just drawn my attention, then faded from memory. A small pang of envy said, "He can afford to buy all the books he wants." A little glow of appreciation said, "He's prosperous; how wonderful that he chooses to indulge in books."

We were still talking about books and seed and plant conservation and a hundred other topics when I looked at the clock on the kitchen wall. It was nearly 5:00.

"I have to leave," I said. "Maggie and my cousin are probably wondering about me and I don't want them to worry."

Ben looked disappointed. "Will you come back tomorrow?" he asked. "If I help out in the morning I think Ernest will give me some more time off."

"Tell you what," I said. "I'll fix a picnic lunch for us and be out about noon. I'll meet you in the grove of trees. Be there at 12:30 sharp!"

Ben nodded enthusiastically and we headed out to the farmyard where Max had been cooling his tires all day under an old box elder tree. As I opened the door to get in, Ben put his arms around me. Without hesitation, my arms went around him. Our goodbye kiss was the kind that stops the brain as well as the breath.

"Come back in the house!" Ben said, tightening his hold.

Working against every natural instinct, I pulled away and slid behind the wheel. "See you tomorrow noon!" I said.

Driving away, I looked at him in the rear view mirror and I could see he was trying to compose himself to greet Ernest, who was walking tentatively across the yard. "He feels the same way I do!" I crowed to myself.

Now and then since Arthur's death, I had crossed paths with some man who had thrown my usually steady equilibrium off balance but damage had been avoided. For the last few years I had recognized these occurrences for the hard to rationalize infatuations they were.

"Two-week burns," I called them in my mind, knowing on some level that even if one was more of a "two-month burn," I was going to eventually opt out of any involvement.

Ben was no infatuation, no "two-week burn." Without reservation, I wanted him in every way more than I'd ever wanted anyone in my entire life.

Sixteen

MAGGIE AND EMILY, particularly Emily, were icy when I got back. They had had a full day of Sunday services in the old home church, plus a pursuit of deceased relatives through a roster of area cemeteries. Maggie was annoyed with me for not being there to help dilute Emily's family history mania while Emily was irritated by my apparently lukewarm interest in our roots.

I had to placate them both by extolling my renewed interest in high school nostalgia. This Emily could understand and she thawed, throwing in a few anecdotes from her own class reunions. Maggie was not amused.

"Why him and why now?" she asked, as soon as we were alone. She knew the only way she could get into my head was by asking questions.

"Because," I answered, "someone like him was always there in the back of my mind. Then, 20 years ago, I stopped believing anyone like that could exist and quit looking for him. But he did exist and I have to see where this is going!"

Maggie groaned. She thought this required rough handling, I knew. I braced myself for one of her unvarnished opinions.

"Be careful," she said, in tones she would never use with one of her clients. "Don't get yourself into a situation you can't back out of by chasing some guy you think was meant to be. They're all just people who pee standing up. Women die a thousand deaths trying to capture and hang onto a 'one and only.' I hear it every day in my work."

Dear Maggie. I love her the way I love my sons but I know her life education is still incomplete, no matter how much information she gets from Out There.

Her both-feet-on-the-ground relationship with Jack is rarer than she realizes. They may not share political and cultural interests but they take care of one another more than almost any couple I've known.

Then, they mutually lavish that caring on rescued animals. Lecturing me about looking for a "one and only" is downright ridiculous.

"Don't worry," I said to her cautions. "I'm not chasing him. Please understand, I couldn't bear it if this isn't mutual. It just feels right. If I find out that it's simply a projection of my own feelings, I'll just consider it one hell of a high school reunion and you can tease me about it every year from now on!"

THE NEXT MORNING I did some quick shopping for picnic supplies. Emily graciously loaned me a hamper and I packed it, re-packed my suitcase, and stowed both in Max's trunk. "Be careful," said Maggie. "Don't confuse wanting to get laid with love."

It was shortly after 12:00 when I drove into the farmyard. That meant I had less than 20 minutes to set up before Ben would head toward the timber.

Lugging the picnic hamper and a blanket across pastures, I was soon into the trees and out of sight of the rest of the farm. There was no time for reconsideration of what I intended to do. I would be returning to Charlotte in a very few days and, before Ben and I parted, I wanted to know as much about him—about us—as possible. Realizing that, I was about to take a shortcut approach.

UNBUTTONING AND SHRUGGING OUT OF MY SHIRT, I placed it partly under a rock that lay beside the creek, leaving a good part of it in plain sight. One of its sleeves just missed the water.

A few trees later, I stepped out of my shorts and carefully hung them from a tree branch that swung over the path.

My bra draped nicely over a blackberry bush and my panties made a concluding statement a few feet before the little clearing where we had talked the day before.

Kicking off my sandals, I spread out the blanket and sat down with my arms clasped around my knees and my back turned away from the path, waiting and waiting as my heart raced.

Moments later, I felt Ben's arms around me and knew he was on his knees behind me. I felt him rise and sensed, rather than heard, his clothing fall to the ground.

He turned me then and our lovemaking was as sudden and primitive as might have been a coupling on this same ground a thousand years before. When it was over, we lay quietly in one another's arms.

"You came back," said Ben. "Don't leave again."

He wasn't simply referring to today and tomorrow, I knew. "I won't," I promised. There was no need for either of us to say anything else.

Lying in this old woods, with the sun filtering through the trees and the meadowlarks repeating their songs over and over in the surrounding fields, we made love again, more slowly. Silently, we did all the things the day and the place and our discovery of one another made perfect.

IT WAS WELL INTO THE AFTERNOON when we dressed. Ben quietly gathered up my belongings and brought it all to me with a kiss. We had our picnic at last, then folded up the blanket and headed back to the house.

There wouldn't be a lot of conversation, even later. Ben acknowledged my small suitcase with a smile when I pulled it from Max's grasp and we walked into the kitchen where, just the day before, we had compared notes on a dozen subjects. We knew we had a lot more to say but also knew that this day was set apart.

I called Maggie, begging her indulgence for my absence. Resigned, she gave me her blessing.

When dark fell, we were in Ben's room, in his narrow bed. We went to sleep in one another's arms.

Seventeen

"WE'D BETTER GO to Ratchford today," Ben said, as a kind of after-thought, approximately an hour after we awoke.

Peering out the window, I saw what he'd seen while on his way to the 1960s-era bathroom down the hall. It was drizzling outside, always a good time for farmers to catch up on town errands. My thoughts flashed to Max. No problem; his top was up.

Returning to the bedroom, rubbing dry with a towel that had seen better days, Ben added, "We need to get some groceries. I need to stop at the bank and we can eat dinner in town. You haven't seen our local bistro! First, I'll go help Ernest out for a couple of hours, then I'll bring the truck up to the house and we can go."

He left for the barn and I sloshed gingerly in an elderly bathtub that exhibited the residue of several years of neglect. "Later," I promised, addressing the tired enamel, "I'll put you into respectable shape."

Pulling on jeans, a tee and sandals, I went down the hall and looked at the big bedroom Ben's parents had occupied.

Hoping their departed spirits and Ben's present one would forgive me, I checked the closets and dresser drawers, searching for extra sheets. All the storage spaces were neat but crammed full of things that badly needed to be sorted and given away. A bottom bureau drawer had what I was looking for and I pulled out sheets and pillowcases.

"Not the freshest after all these years!" I thought, and carried them downstairs to the washer and dryer that stood in an alcove off the dining room. Tonight we would sleep in a full-sized bed on clean sheets. Ben's single bed had been adequate at the end of a day of exhaustive lovemaking but I could think of future activity that would benefit from additional space.

BEN PULLED THE TRUCK UP TO THE BACK DOOR around 11:00. Rain was spilling from the downspouts and didn't look as if it would end for hours. The ride to town was the first time in years I'd really looked attentively at this farm country that I had left behind more than 30 years before. Two beautiful horses were waiting out the weather under a tree in a nearby pasture.

57

"Yours?" I asked.

"Nope," said Ben. That's not our land over here and I don't take time for a horse. Would you like to have one? I'll get one for you, only you have to take care of it."

'That sounds like what I used to say to my boys when they asked for a dog," I said.

My mind registered his comment seconds later. He was so matter of fact, taking it for granted that I'd be part of his life and his farm from now on.

Although that was my thinking, as well, I resolved that he wasn't going to get by with such a casual declaration of intent. First, however, I had to acknowledge a basic truth. Ben's farm was part of his person. There would be no alternative choices or compromises about where we lived. He might love me and care for me with all his heart and soul, but for him to dwell anywhere except on his farm would mean becoming half a man. Part of returning his love was accepting that without question.

BEFORE PARKING ON RATCHFORD'S MAIN DRAG, Ben gave me a quick tour of the town. What had changed since my high school graduation? Um. There was a new football field with better bleachers. The schoolhouse had an addition to accommodate a student base now drawn from a wider area. The Congregational church had a new fellowship hall where the old parsonage had stood. There were houses now where there had been streets that dead-ended into pastures. Their occupants worked in larger towns nearby, Ben said. It seemed to me that the major change was in the small town amenities that no longer existed. The drugstore where my father had sold cough syrup, birthday cards and Ponds Cold Cream was gone. A grocery store with a parking lot replaced three Main Street stores of my youth. There no longer was a furniture store, a downtown implement dealership or a newspaper office.

"Are there more stores on some other street?" I carefully questioned.

Ben laughed. "We're down to basics," he said. "Everybody drives to Des Moines or Newton or Grinnell. People who have jobs in those places shop there, too, when they get off work."

While I waited in the truck, he went into the Ratchford Savings Bank to do whatever business needed attention. He was back within minutes and we walked over to the Main Street Restaurant. It was pretty well filled up with farmers and when we entered there was a split-second hush with all heads turned toward us. They all knew Ben, of course. On other days they would probably have greeted him with a low-key wisecrack and moved over to make room for him. Today, because of me, several nodded gravely, then turned back to their talk.

Ben and I took a booth over against the far wall. Iowa country courtesy would, I knew, keep the other patrons from looking at us again. To do so would be considered rude by some deep seated rural code of behavior. I also knew that when they later ate supper with their families their tongues would wag and the women folk would take care of disseminating the information about who had been in town on that rainy day.

The woman who came to take our order looked as if she might be eking out her Social Security check. On the other hand, she could be the restaurant owner. Small town Iowa is an egalitarian place.

"Hello, Ben," she said, while nevertheless looking at me. She added, "I guess you're Janilee Jasper."

"Aha," I thought. "I must be aging very well if I'm recognized from high school days."

"How did you know?" I asked, getting ready to hear some flattering comments.

"Easy. You could just be your mother sitting there!"

Oh.

SUDDENLY I NEEDED COMFORT FOOD and ordered the pork tenderloin, mashed potatoes and mixed vegetables.

"I know zip about these people," I thought, looking at the group of farmers. When I was living here as a kid, my mind had been in far-off places and centuries. These days I was up-to-date on the immense environmental problems afoot in the world, but I didn't have the slightest idea if these people in this room believed in global warming or the critical problems with ground water or if they, nowadays, continued to dump chemical fertilizers in their fields or stuff their animals with hormones. I didn't even know for sure where Ben stood on all these things.

Some of that I said out loud to him.

"Not criticizing," I hastily added. "I see the solar windmills and know about the pros and cons of ethanol. But I've spent so many years with corporate suits that the people I grew up with are strangers!"

Ben didn't seem concerned. "You'll catch on," was his meager, Iowa-like response.

But I wasn't giving up my scrutiny. The presidential hopefuls of every election cycle were often out here courting these quiet Iowa people and the omnipresent hopefuls were not merely expatriates like me; they were from different tribes altogether. What could a native-born Iowan possibly think of a New Yorker with numerous marriages and big city ways? Southerners who spoke of heartfelt emotions while harboring a deceitful soul. A black man who did not seem to be a black man? Westerners whose pores and womenfolk exuded money?

"How come," I asked Ben, "with all these presidential candidates running around here, there aren't any local Favorite Sons?"

"Ought to be," said Ben. "If we had one, what do you think he'd be like?"

"Or *she,*" I said. "Not too talkative. Germanic roots. Name something like 'Ivan Schroder.'"

"A farmer?" asked Ben.

"Grew up on a farm," I fabricated, "but he has to be an attorney. Got his law degree at Iowa U. or Ames."

"Finances?" asked Ben.

"Made his money representing farm industries," I said. "And his father…"

"Otto Schroder!" Ben happily interjected.

"Old Otto," I said, leaning forward confidentially, "had a string of farms he inherited from homesteading ancestors but he also owned most of the bank stock in several county seat towns!"

"What about Ivan's wife?" asked Ben.

"Karen Schroder! The Midwest's answer to Martha Stewart," I fantasized. "Graduated from Ames. Had her own radio show up until he was elected Senator and they went to Washington. I think she specialized in programs about church cookbooks and got women guests in to talk about their favorite pot luck recipes and upcoming fund raisers."

"Let's run him!" said Ben. "He'll take the Iowa caucus in a landslide!"

"Don't you already have someone kind of like that in Congress?" I asked.

"Doesn't have Ivan's charisma!" Ben said, adding, "And nowhere near his family background!"

All of this was alternated with mouthfuls of potatoes and gravy. Meals had been sketchy since Saturday night's reunion dinner and both of us were hungry. I jotted a mental note that Ben needed more and better food than canned tuna and thrown-together picnic fare.

Verna—that was the waitress's name—left a cryptic note at our table about what we'd eaten and Ben went up to the cash register to pay the bill. As we left, I wondered if the heads would again swivel to watch us as we walked out the door. "Get used to it," I thought.

True to Iowa etiquette, the farmers at the next table acknowledged our departure with quick little bobs of their heads and Ben did a swift return bob. I was no part of this, but I was aware of a slight, very slight, sideways movement of the farmers' eyes toward me. An assessment would be made, for sure, and passed on to their wives.

Eighteen

WE DROVE TO THE GROCERY STORE and, except for adding a head of lettuce and some grapes, I played a passive role. While Ben filled the cart, I wandered over to the liquor section feeling like a tourist. I'd never seen booze of all varieties, from Scotch to vodka, sold in a grocery store. The sheer novelty made me want to buy a case of Scotch just because I could have it rung up with bread and beans. I realized that another thing I didn't know about Ben was if he drank anything stronger than ginger ale. Personally, I liked a drink in the evening before dinner and Ben was going to have to get used to it the same way I was going to have to get used to co-existing with a herd of cattle. I added two bottles of Merlot to the grocery cart, avoiding the curious glance of a woman whose grocery cart was stalled between the paper plates and the potato chips.

"Is she watching me?" I asked myself, and decided that I was being paranoid.

When we got back to the farm, Ben demonstrated an ability to adjust swiftly to a traditional him and her household. Leaving me to guess where the newly bought groceries should go, he was quickly off to the farmyard to check in with the long-suffering Ernest.

I took the clean sheets out of the dryer and went upstairs to make up the double bed. If I came back to Iowa to stay, I mused, would this be my future? Unloading groceries and making beds? Trailing Ben into Farm Bureau events in Des Moines?

If only I understood these people! Crossing culture lines is not for the faint of heart. When Arthur and I were married and settled down in Charlotte, I wasn't comfortable for a long time. The Minnesota-born wife of one of Milton's friends suggested a seminar called "The South for Non-Southerners," which I attended and enjoyed. Since most of the participants had come from other parts of the country to join local corporations, the discussion was lively and relevant. Unlike them, I got to stay at home in my fancy gated community acquiring an acceptable Southern veneer at my own pace. There was a lot to learn, much of it good. My native Iowa code of manners was eventually sanded off and polished to a more silken finish.

When I started my first job, my department boss baited me relentlessly. A New York native, he insultingly edited everything I wrote, employing long, long red-ink slashes, and calling me "Fargo."

This was a far cry from the Midwestern male diffidence, real or feigned, to which I was accustomed. My country-bred inclinations would have been to lay into him with barnyard curses. Instead, one day I invited him and Donna, his wife, to dinner. For once, I was gleeful about the routine that the guards at our community's gate would put him through.

He was, of course, simmering when he and Donna arrived in the circular driveway in front of our big Colonial house but he said not a word. He just sat watching me with eyes wide open as Arthur, a true Southern gentleman, gently courted both him and his wife. I served dinner, making sure plenty of Midwestern cookbook specialties were laid out on Arthur's grandmother's best china. It was Southern hospitality garnished with Iowa calories and his wife liked it, even if he didn't know what to do or say or how to handle his immense damask napkin.

Donna probably told him what to think when they drove home and after that he kept his opinions to himself when we discussed my work. His main focus centered, going forward, on getting me out of his department. Ultimately he wrote a nice evaluation suggesting he had trained me well and that was helpful in getting me out of technical writing and into the regular communications department. Donna, when our paths crossed at company-wide events, always greeted me like a dear old friend—an attitude I didn't deserve.

Subsequently, I made it a practice to observe the styles of a wide range of other managers and executives. I was damned if I'd be caught off guard again but also determined to find a mode of operation I could adapt as my own. I saw some managers bluster, some sulk, some seduce (mentally, not necessarily physically), some achieve success through collecting smart women who would do excellent work while not expecting much reward by way of salary or advancement. A maltreated but adoring woman would be impotent when dropped for a younger and more attractive protégé.

Then, there were the blessed few, the best, managers who made stars of those reporting to them whenever possible. I aspired to become like them and appreciated the quality when I observed it in leaders in all venues of life.

The most valuable lesson I learned was that, wherever one lives, day-to-day social and employment success is best achieved by judicious reflection and temperate action. Neither came naturally to me but practice eased my life considerably, at work and at home.

Now, in Ratchford, it would be like starting over. I was back to my roots but they no longer were familiar. This rural environment was not the oasis of a Midwestern university or even the carrot and stick milieu of a corporation. These local people were real, they had agendas I couldn't identify, and they still, after all these years, didn't fit any communication or motivation patterns that I understood. One thing for sure, they hated pretension with every fiber of their being. Could I find my own niche? Would there be a place for me in this Iowa of my youth?

Nineteen

I FINISHED MAKING THE BIG BED and put together an evening meal for us. It seemed I was quieter than I'd been before because Ben looked puzzled and said, "A penny for your thoughts!"

Brushing aside the hesitations that had crept into my mind, I asked him to refresh my memory about Iowa weather in general and last winter's in particular. It wasn't a soothing topic as he described 20 below zero temperatures, power outages and snow drifts that closed the roads into town.

Semi-enjoying my horror, he capped it with, "Of course, warmer weather isn't always great, either. It can get hotter than it ever thought of being down South. How does 110 degrees sound to you? And don't forget, every summer at least one Iowa town gets wiped out by a tornado!"

WE WENT TO BED EARLY and my apprehensions were lost for the time being. The bigger bed was a decided success and helped wipe out my afternoon wish for a seminar on "Rural Iowa for Non-Iowans." Lust, it seemed, was not a negative trait when partners matched.

As we finally dozed off, Ben said sleepily that he'd have to get up early and put in the morning with Ernest. Then he'd come back for lunch and in the late afternoon we'd go to Des Moines for dinner and talk about re-modeling the house.

I slept. At some hour, I dreamed I was the defendant in a Supreme Court case. A taciturn Ernest announced, "All rise!" and nine Justices filed in looking at me. They were all wearing bib overalls and seed corn caps. There was one lady Justice and she looked at me the hardest.

She had Caroline Allan's face.

WHEN THAT LADY DROVE INTO THE FARM-YARD the next morning, I didn't know whether to address her as "Mrs. Allan," "Caroline," or "Your Honor."

She'd been "Mrs. Allan" when I was in high school, although I had called her other things in my head. Seeing her at the reunion had called up grim recollections. The woman I now saw getting out of her Buick was decades older than the woman who had taught my high school cooking and sewing classes but she was, if anything, even scarier.

RATCHFORD HIGH DIDN'T HAVE a wide assortment of class subjects in bygone days and the required courses outnumbered the electives. "Shop" for boys was a must, as was one year of "Homemaking" for girls. In my freshman year I bumbled through a semester of cooking, which included detailed instructions for canning tomatoes. The girls who came from farms already knew all about that and one of them even gave a mini-lecture on what kind of peaches were easiest to can. To this day, when I consider peaches at the supermarket I ask myself, "Are these cling-stone or free-stone?"

Mother wasn't a particularly good cook, herself, and had no patience with me as a kitchen assistant. I knew how to make cupcakes and frosting and Jell-O salad, but my repertoire ended there. In cooking classes, Mrs. Allan suggested that all of us girls try out one new recipe. She would buy the chief ingredients from the Home Economics budget and we would make only enough for a little taste for all of us. I don't recall what the other girls chose but assume they proposed dishes that would have practical applications.

When it was my turn, I said I'd like to make ham soufflé. Nobody I knew, young or old, made or ate soufflé, but it sounded sophisticated. Mrs. Allan raised a skinny, penciled eyebrow.

"Ham is an expensive ingredient," she said, and later supplied a packet of bologna. I ground it up, just as the recipe required, but bologna isn't a good substitute for ham. Plus, the soufflé fell just as soufflés are wont to do. The "little taste" that everyone got resulted in puckered mouths and wrinkled noses. My semester grade was "C," a catastrophe I had never experienced.

However, it was sewing that left me totally frustrated and unhappy about my lack of ability to turn out a satisfactory product. We all had to make a sample scrapbook of every kind of seam, placket and stitch that could possibly rear its miserable contour in any pattern whatsoever. Only when we finished our sample scrapbook could we cut out and sew an actual garment. I was a dud. Two or three kind young women sneaked samples into my scrapbook and finally, thanks to them, it was finished. We were to keep these scrapbooks forever, as an aid in future sewing; I took mine home and threw it in the trash.

It all came to a head the last week of school. The first and second year sewing classes were to present an evening style show and tea to which our mothers and the other women of the community had been invited. This was a big deal for Caroline Allan, an annual event at which she demonstrated high hostessing and teaching skills and collected suitable praise from the people whose accolades she valued.

The girls were each going to model outfits they had made. The high school gymnasium was decorated with crepe paper streamers and spring flowers. The Shop boys had set up a white picket fence with a gate. Every young woman was to emerge, in turn, from a curtained-off area and walk as gracefully as possible down the fence line, come through the gate and stroll among the guests. There would be a moderator who would stand at a microphone describing each garment as it was presented. Against what had to be her deepest wishes, Mrs. Allan chose me to be that moderator.

Her choice was, I smugly thought, inevitable. Despite my lack of social skill with peers, I had already acquired something of a reputation in the community for being capable on my feet in front of an audience. My mother had, after all, set me in front of church groups and County Fair crowds since age three. In the early years she chose my material, usually light, humorous pieces that featured a child's-eye view of the grownup world. By the age of ten, the sound of adult laughter coaxed into existence by my performance was a turn-on that had me hooked. With age, my "readings" got more sophisticated. By my own choice, I was up to essays from *New Yorker Magazine* by the time I was a senior. To her credit, Mother never pointed out how unsuitable these pieces were for a farming community.

Because no other kid in town had been trained to memorize such monologues, I continued to get lots of invitations to deliver them in front of Eastern Star assemblies and other community events. No other kid in town would have wanted to be singled out in that way, either, but I didn't know that; in my innocence, I thrived on it and could only muse on the mystery of why I could confidently stand on my feet in front of audiences, yet be mute in a group of five kids my own age.

ON THE AFTERNOON OF THE STYLE SHOW the home economics classroom was empty except for two people—Caroline Allan and me. She was putting final touches on the little sandwiches and cakes that would be served at the tea party. And I was sitting in front of a sewing machine still trying to finish the green cotton jumper I was obliged to wear as I moderated the show. I would never, it seemed, master the zipper installation.

As I held up the simple garment, I was overcome by its lack of perfection and by how downright dowdy it was. With a shriek that must have curled my teacher's toes, I tore the jumper, which opened down the side, from top to bottom. Too proud to burst into tears, I threw it on the floor and tore off to the girls' rest room to cry in solitude.

When I returned, shamefaced, to the sewing room, I saw Caroline Allan at the sewing machine repairing the damage. Without a word, for the next hour she worked to remake the destroyed garment, setting a row of buttons to camouflage the compromised zipper placket.

When she was finished, she handed the jumper to me. "Go home and iron it," she said, lip curling. "Do you think you can manage that?"

It didn't look half-bad that evening as I stood before Ratchford's matrons narrating the style show. At least two people complimented me on the creativity of the white buttons marching down my side. My mother, who knew nothing of the afternoon's debacle, was gratified, as she expected to be.

Mrs. Allan gave me a D for the semester, the lowest grade I ever got but one that was well-deserved. The following year all the other girls in my class chose a second year of homemaking class as an elective. At Mr. Door's suggestion, I took Greg shorthand instead. Mrs. Allan and I never again acknowledged one another's presence until we were trapped into it last Saturday night at the ninety-ninth Ratchford alumni reunion.

What I had wanted to make her understand was that in my grownup years I had developed an enthusiasm for gourmet cooking as well as some skills with fabric. Astonishingly often, something I thought I hadn't learned in her home economics class *had* been learned, after all, and lurked in my brain until time for its retrieval.

NOW SHE WAS HERE. Here in this place I hoped to call home in the very near future. Could she ever bring herself to be a friend? Walking outside to greet her, I decided to play it the corporate way.

"Good morning," I called, in my most cordial visiting-the-field-office voice. "I'm at a loss as to what to call you now that I'm all grown up. May I call you Caroline?"

"Of course!" she said, with just the slightest wisp of reserve. "I saw your car when I came from town just now, and thought I'd stop and say 'Hello.'"

No doubt Caroline Allan had been observing Max for the last three days, but I didn't care and was nearly sure that Ben wouldn't, either. More to the point, would I now have to invite her inside? Yes, I would. I hadn't returned to Iowa to flout its traditions.

"Please disregard Ben's housekeeping," I said, holding the screen door wide for her to enter. "It's pretty much a typical bachelor house, I'm afraid. But I know where the coffee pot is and would love to have you join me in a cup."

While I measured out the coffee, Caroline examined the room with avid interest. "Isn't this a dear old house?" she said. "If Ben ever wants to do it over, I have a file cabinet chock full of wonderful ideas! I'm almost sure there are interesting walls behind walls and floors under floors. This place could be just like a magazine cover!"

"Oh," I thought. "Is this Caroline Allan's ultimate dream? Would I have to consult her about ways to remodel the farmhouse to make up for the green jumper?" Time to change the subject.

"You know what I wonder about?" I said, very brightly. "I happen to be a gardening enthusiast and I'm curious if there were ever interesting shrubs or flowers here. I saw the row of peony bushes and somebody had to have gone to the trouble of planting them."

Caroline jumped to her feet. I had evidently hit on something we had in common. For the time being, at least, we stopped two-stepping around one another.

"Ben's grandmother loved flowers!" she said. "His mother told me all about how her mother-in-law had experimented with some unusual shrubs and perennials. Let's go see if we can find any traces of them!"

Leaving the coffeepot to fend for itself, the two of us actually raced outside together and began poking around with enthusiasm.

To not much avail, however. Outside of a couple of malnourished and non-blooming lilacs, plus a scraggly honeysuckle, there was little of botanical interest.

At one side of the house a flat, round cement slab caught my attention. I pushed at it tentatively with one foot but it didn't budge.

"The old cistern!" said Caroline. "I wonder if it still holds water." Stooping, she moved it to one side.

I tried not to register surprise, but thought, "Yo, Mama!" and took a good look at Caroline Allan in her seniorhood.

When she was my teacher, she had stood nearly six feet tall—a goodly stature for a woman but not truly extraordinary for a healthy farm girl. Probably in her 40s at that time, she must now be into her 70s. She had added girth over the years and could be classified as a strapping big woman—one who could still shove a heavy cement well cover from one place to another despite her years.

Straightening up after pushing the cover back in place, she looked rather disappointed. "It's been filled in!" she said. "I imagine that might have been done for safety reasons when Ben and Karl were little."

While it had been interesting to observe Caroline's little demonstration of strength, our garden inspection was otherwise a flop. I was relieved when she headed for her car. Out of some nether depth came words from my mouth that I had heard from my mother when bidding farewell to guests—words that had lain fallow in my brain along with the intricacies of hemming a garment.

"Don't rush off!" I said.

Caroline wasn't rushing but she was definitely on her way. "Harold will be looking for his dinner," she said. "Bye!"

Whoever Harold was—dog, cat or husband—I silently blessed him and waved goodbye in as neighborly a way as I could muster.

Shortly after I went back into the kitchen, there was a gentle tap at the back door. Ernest stood there, squirming. Refusing an invitation to come inside, he backed to one side to make room for me as I stepped out.

"Ben asked me to tell you he had to run into town for something and to go ahead and eat lunch without him. He'll be back in time to wash up before you go to Des Moines," he said.

I smiled at him. "Okay," I said. "Thanks for telling me, Ernest."

He looked as if he wanted to say something more and I smiled at him again.

"You know," he said, "I just couldn't hardly believe you're Janilee Jasper. I saw you around a couple times when you were a kid. I knew your dad."

There was a little wait. I knew he had more to add.

"Your dad was a fine man. He worked in the drugstore and could fill prescriptions just like that old son-of-a-gun who owned it."

Remembering, Ernest looked as if he had an unpleasant thought.

"Old devil wasn't even from around here. I think he came from someplace over by Ankeny.

"I was real down on my luck back one time after my wife had our middle boy and she was real sick. The doc gave me a prescription for her and I didn't have enough money to pay for it. I took it over to the drugstore and asked that old devil if I could have it on credit and he said, 'No. You're already on the books and you don't look like you're going to pay up any time soon.'

"I felt real bad and went on out of the store and just went across the street and leaned on my truck. I saw that devil of a druggist come out and drive away and wished I had me a slingshot to pop out the front window on his store.

"Your dad come outta the store in a couple minutes with a little sack in his hand and walked over to me. He said, 'Here. I made up that prescription for your wife. Just forget about it. Scrooge don't need to know!'

"He walked away and I called out, 'Much obliged!' to him but I never had a chance to thank him more after I got on my feet because he had his heart attack about that time and died."

I knew how hard it must have been for Ernest to tell me that. True to his roots, this man who could only manage "Much obliged," to someone to whom he felt tremendous gratitude, must have found it even harder to speak to a woman who was a stranger.

He stepped off the porch, but there was one more thing he wanted to say, whatever discomfort it caused him.

"I guess," he added, "you're going to be around quite a bit in the future. I am real glad for Ben and I want you to know that if there is ever anything you need, you can count on me."

Fighting tears, I said, "Thank you, Ernest. I'll remember that and I know my dad would appreciate it!"

Twenty

WITH MUCH OF THE AFTERNOON TO MYSELF before Ben's return, I carried an apple out to the old wooden glider in the front yard and began lining up my thoughts.

Whether or not I loved Ben was not one of the questions to consider. We had much to learn about the every-day parts of one another, but we had connected in some solid way that provided for the differences as well as the similarities that would appear in the future.

Could I return to Ratchford to live? A troubling question, but it was settled by the thought that living without Ben had, with dizzying rapidity, become out of the question.

But how could I live in Ratchford without giving up important parts of myself? That was a deeper problem. The answers would have to be diligently sought and would take time. First of all, of course, I would have to learn to love the farm and, for me, a central part of loving the farm would be feeling comfortable with my immediate home.

Wherever I had lived, over the years, it meant having a garden, and to garden in mid-Iowa was an undisputed blessing. I had been in the habit of telling Southern friends, as they taught me ways to do battle with red clay, that in Iowa one had only to set a wooden chair outside and before long it would sprout roots.

It came down, then, to the house. Could I live in this farmhouse where generations of Ben's family had been conceived, born, brought up, died and been laid out?

Caroline Allan had seemed enthused about its possibilities. For me, after my first look at it, it didn't ring any bells. But then, my eyes had been only for Ben.

Pitching my apple core to a squirrel that had climbed down from one of the big, old trees, I walked slowly around the house, trying to look at it with unbiased eyes.

The last remodeling must have been about the time Ben graduated high school. Wide, white shingle facing and faux shutters had likely been a decent face lift at the time. Both were now the worse for wear as was the front porch which, in its latest incarnation, had probably been a mere repair of a previous porch. A picture window had been punched into one side of the living room and, unfortunately, it was on the side that faced the gravel road, not the side that looked out on peaceful fields.

The back door opened directly into the kitchen, a huge room with appliances marching compulsively around its perimeters. Years ago, a big country table in the center might have extended to gigantic capacity when open, the better to seat threshers, neighbors and huge families. At some point, however, such a table had been supplanted by a lesser-sized chrome set that was short both on character and charm.

The dining and living rooms had each been furnished with matching sets of furniture that were what a local family would have called a "suit," as in "a dining room suit" or a "living room suit." These had perhaps come from a Ratchford furniture emporium, when it had one. Mother, whose taste ran to black walnut Victorian bought at auction, said it was recliners out the front door and coffins out the back door with small town furniture shops.

A room off to the side of the front room might have once been an extra bedroom but now held little beside a daybed and a rocking chair. It was easy to envision a television set, a sewing machine, a piano, all things that once might have been there and could be again if they were wanted.

Climbing the stairs, I skipped Ben's room and the bigger bedroom. The bathroom, in its current state, was a disaster in more ways than the soap scum that clung to the tub. When it had last undergone revision, the lady of the house—it was undoubtedly Ben's mother—had chosen pink.

Pink tile. A pink tub. A pink toilet. A pink lavatory. A farm wife's self-indulgence in a world where what worked for the all-male farm household in which she lived didn't necessarily work for her.

"Good for her," I thought. "I hope she loved it and didn't mind the teasing!"

That left one room that had not yet been examined—Karl's. He'd been dead for quite a long time. Yet, according to Ben, his room had simply been left as it was and closed up.

When I had asked about it, a day or so ago, Ben just shrugged. "That whole thing was so hard for Mother," he said, "I don't think she had the heart to go through his things. After the funeral she tidied it up some and put his clothes away in drawers, but it finally got to be like a healed-over wound. She didn't go in there and brood, that I know of. She just let it go, since we didn't need the space."

Now, I opened the door and took a long, hard look. Like Ben's room, it was a utilitarian space. Good quality linoleum on the floor, a braided rug beside the bed, a smallish roll-top desk, closed, and a dresser. It was the material on the walls that crashed into my consciousness.

Religious pictures, mostly unframed posters with biblical figures, dominated a good share of the wall area.

"Ben didn't say anything about Karl being an evangelical Christian," I mused. Ben was not, to my knowledge, and had mentioned that his parents had been members of the local Congregational church.

But Congregationalists are not given to emotionally intense religious icons, as far as I knew, and these pictures were intense.

Christ crucified, to be sure, but a Christ in such agony! His crown of thorns pressed down, his wounds bleeding in heavy rivulets, the eyes of this Christ on Karl's wall stared into mine with such anguished fervor that I found myself shrinking back toward the hall.

Over and over, the image was replicated in other pictures, interspersed now and again with a horizontal cross and Roman soldiers maniacally pounding nails into pale hands and feet.

A poster above the foot of the bed pictured a many-tentacled beast, the kind of Revelation imagery I'd seen a time or two on a gaudy pamphlet handed out by a representative of some zealous denomination.

A ferocious Satan, his twisted lips drooling blood, threatened from the closet door. Curious, I looked at everything more intently, fighting an urge to run away. The posters seemed to have some sort of three-dimensional quality because the closer scrutiny revealed a quality at first unobserved. When the summer afternoon light rays struggled through the grimy, fly-specked window and glanced off the posters, the images appeared to flicker and undulate in some peculiar way. The monster seemed to wave its tentacles menacingly in my direction. The Roman soldier looked up, sneering, from his crucifixion task, and his curling lips all but mouthed, "You're next!"

It was a macabre collection that seemed to worsen every second and it scared me to the point of panic. Childishly, I could have sworn the lid of the roll top desk began to move up and down and the closet door begin to thrust outward as if something within was forcing it open.

This man—this Karl who had owned this collection—what had he done? Or what had been done *to* him to make him seek companionship with these terrible things? Choking back a scream, I backed out, slamming the door. Never again would I go into Karl's old room alone. It was no wonder it had been left untouched. To reclaim it, taking away these fanatic versions of the Crucifixion and the threat of hell-fire that snarled from the visage of Revelations monsters, would be enough to induce a year of nightmares. I wasn't going to report this episode to Ben, lest he question my sanity, but something would have to be done if I was ever going to live in this house and sleep in the room down the hall.

Twenty-One

BY THE TIME BEN WAS BACK from the "town" errands that Ernest had reported, I was dressed for Des Moines. Since I hadn't packed what I'd consider going-out-to-dinner clothes, the white jeans and green shirt I'd worn to the Saturday night reunion dinner would have to do. More importantly, I now harbored an unyielding resolution or two that I needed to communicate to Ben, tough as that might turn out to be.

Ben changed into khakis and sport shirt, with a sport jacket tossed over that. When he handed me into the pickup for the 25-mile trip to Des Moines, I had to battle a burst of euphoria which, if I gave in to it, would have me giggling like a teenager. It was a beautiful June evening, my man was someone to be proud of, and we were on our way to the Big City!

My travels for my company and a few vacations had taken me to a fair number of well-known cities. I'd been to London, New York City, Rome, Budapest, Istanbul, San Francisco and Berlin, to recall a few. I'd been awed by some of them and could later compare notes with other travelers as to cuisine and points of interest. Yet, the excitement I'd felt when visiting any of them had contrasted weakly with what it had been like, as a young teenager, to go to Des Moines.

Money was tight at our house. My father's salary at the drugstore was modest; we were not a farm family so we had to buy our provisions and make payments on our house. If we needed more than food, we went to one of the small county seat towns around us to shop. Close-by though it was, Des Moines was too big to be a destination of choice for our simple purchases.

Until I reached my teen years, that is, and Mother decided I was going to be as much of a fashion plate as she could manage. She had grown up very poor on a heavily mortgaged farm, had gone through her own school years ragged and ashamed, and was determined that no daughter of hers would know such misery.

No matter that casual dress was becoming more acceptable. She would have none of it. Off to Des Moines we would go, spring and fall, to its prime department store with its selection of "junior" fashions.

In Des Moines there were women who smoked openly; there

were people of other colors than pale white; there were movie theaters with thick carpets and brilliant chandeliers; there was a tea room in Younkers Department Store where the serving women wore crisp black uniforms and frilly white aprons. Mother favored a Bishop's Cafeteria in another downtown spot that had a selection of elegantly presented foods. If we felt especially festive, we paid the two cents extra for a cloth napkin. Choosing a salad, main course and dessert was a major excitement. Cheery people at the end of the line carried trays to linen-clad tables as customers scurried behind; I always felt a little guilty about that particular amenity.

Breathless at the sophistication and grandeur, always, I frequently endangered my mental stability by removing myself to an outside observer perspective. From there, I could admire myself living an unbelievably fabulous adventure in which I was the chief character.

It could be said that, for me, Des Moines amounted to an out-of-body experience.

But, from the time I graduated high school until now, I had not been back. Now, here we were—going to Des Moines!

THE PLACE WAS LARGER NOW, yet it could never attain a size that matched my teen-age impressions. As Ben and I drove through its outskirts and toward the center of town, he pointed out the many advances and attractions. The city was obviously on a level with other state capitols but no late-vintage improvements could raise it higher than the image I carried in my mind.

When we entered the restaurant, it was evident Ben was familiar with it and had made reservations. While we didn't quite have it to ourselves, it was not particularly busy. A small group of men in suits and ties held down a table in one corner.

Ben ordered drinks for us and as we raised our glasses to one another, he cleared his throat. What was he going to say, I wondered, hoping that one of my resolves—to clarify how we were going to proceed with our lives—would be addressed by him before I would have to do so.

Just then, the small group of professionally garbed men in the corner got up to leave. A big, blond man a few years younger than his companions approached our table. "Hello, Ben," he said, nodding with the brisk courtesy of someone who was then going to engage in conversation with someone else. He turned to me and held out his hand.

"Janilee," he said, "I want to welcome you to Iowa. Ivan Schroder, here!"

Ivan Schroder. Ivan Schroder? Where had I heard that name? In Ratchford's Main Street Restaurant, when Ben and I had eaten there yesterday! But it wasn't a name Ben had come up with; it was the fictitious name I had tossed out as my Favorite Son, "*Ivan Schroder!*"

"Ivan" handed me a small package. "Just to make sure your return is all it should be!" he said. Then he turned and he and his group strode out the restaurant door.

"Who *was* that?" I demanded of Ben. "And don't tell me it's any Favorite Son. You know him!"

"Not important," said Ben. "You'll meet him some other time. What's in the package?"

Tearing off the silver-colored outer wrapping, I found a little blue velvet box and in the box a beautiful engagement ring. "Will you stay in Iowa and marry me?" Ben asked.

And after that there was so much to say that the subject of "Ivan's" identity didn't come up again that evening. Obviously, it was a joke conceived and engineered by Ben but I'd consider it later. For now, I thought it was nice that I wasn't going to be a kept woman. Not that it would have deterred me. If Ben hadn't proposed, I'd have lived with him without benefit of clergy, even if we had to make our home under that rickety little bridge down the road from his farm. Still, the present alternative seemed to make both of us incredibly happy.

By the time we finally managed to eat some of the excellent meal that Ben had ordered, the subject of my other resolve came up.

"What do you want to do about remodeling the house?" Ben asked.

I swallowed. This was going to be very, very hard.

"Ben," I said, "I don't want to live in that house. No matter how much we did to change it, it would always seem strange to me, as if something there doesn't welcome me. I'm so sorry. Does it matter so much to you that we should rethink all of our plans?"

"What do you think we should do about it?" Ben asked.

Here came my greed demon. "I want a new house!" I said. "I want to build a new house that has everything that goes into green construction—solar panels, recycled materials, tankless water heating, you name it! A house that is as environmentally tuned as today's technology allows, from one end to the other and absolutely gorgeous besides! If that sounds too costly, there is at least one place in Minnesota that makes modular homes that are built green."

Ben threw his head back and laughed so hard and so long that I began to worry. Was he laughing at me? Did he find me so ridiculous that I had unwittingly become a comedian in his eyes? Worse, was he so upset at what I said that he could only maintain his equilibrium by laughing?

"Janilee," he said, finally, "I've been wondering how to break it to you that I'd like to do just that! I thought possibly you had set your heart on making an up-to-date Tara out of the old farm house and was prepared to talk you out of it! I've been sick of that drafty old dump for years!"

And then we talked and talked—about my beautiful new ring and his afternoon search to find it, about what an environmentally up-to-date Iowa farmhouse might look like, about when we would get married and where, about my boys coming to visit, about the return trip to Charlotte that I would have to make on Saturday, about how soon I could settle my affairs and get back to Iowa. We suddenly realized that it was late, that people had arrived, occupied other tables in the restaurant and gone again, that the waiters were shifting nervously in the corner because the place was about to close for the evening and we hadn't signaled our intent to leave.

We drove back to the farm and the rest of the night was as glorious as the preceding hours. It was also bittersweet because the next day would be our last together until I got back from the Carolinas. Maggie and I would have to drive to Wisconsin on Friday so I could fly back to Charlotte on Saturday.

"Two weeks!" said Ben. "You have two weeks to quit your job and do what you need to do about closing down your house or putting it on the market. Fly to Des Moines in two weeks and we'll start house planning."

I could do that, but I had some questions for Ben.

"What are you going to do about all that stuff in the farmhouse?" I asked. "Every drawer and shelf and closet is crammed full of things that belonged to someone who doesn't need it anymore."

"Sorry," said Ben. "I don't know usable stuff from trash. You're going to have to help. After you come back we'll go at it as hard as you want."

Agreed. It could be fun, sort of—as long as I didn't have to tackle his dead brother's room with its frenzied images of torture victims and sadistic religious zealots.

THE NEXT DAY, Thursday, we walked the farm hand in hand. Once in a while we caught a glimpse of Ernest beaming down at us from a tractor and smiled back at him. We took a picnic back to the grove of trees and made love in their sheltering shade. We scratched house plans in the gravel road.

Ben stood forlornly in the farmyard on Friday morning. I kissed him goodbye for a long time before turning Max around for the trip over to Emily's to pick up Maggie. As I had done only a few days before, I watched him in the rear view mirror.

"My beautiful Ben," I thought. "I longed for him all my life without knowing it was him, with his mind that meets mine straight on and his body that matches my own and his quirky sense of humor that keeps me alert. He is a thousand times better than I am, but he loves me. We will spend the rest of our days together. Those days won't all be perfect but, because we care so much for one another, they will be more perfect than any days we would have otherwise lived. Are we not as fortunate as life allows any two people to be?"

Book Three: Ben

Dene Hellman

Twenty-Two

IT WAS HARD TO see Janilee leave, driving off in that fancy convertible that made her feel so good. She was returning to the Carolina town where she had spent years living and learning. Maybe when she got there, she'd decide that coming back to Iowa wasn't worth the effort. I had to have faith that in rediscovering one another we had found something unmatchable and that she *would* be back in a couple of weeks.

Two weeks is not long, however, no matter how much I missed her, and there was plenty to do in the meanwhile. I'd missed four days of farm work, which is not a casual thing, even though Ernest had been a good fellow to cover for me. I made a mental note to give him a couple of days off, soon, in case he wanted them. You never can tell about Ernest, though. He has no talent for relaxation. Usually, he'd rather be chasing an ornery old cow than occupied with recreational pursuits.

There were for sure going to be some big changes around here: a new house to build, Janilee's family coming and going, and helping her do whatever it would take to get to feeling part of what is, after all, her home state. We'd probably have to socialize more in the arts scene, to please her, in addition to maintaining my involvement in state environmental and conservation projects. I was going to have to talk to Ernest as soon as possible about hiring some more help on a permanent basis. With all the projects I had in mind, now given even more momentum with Janilee at my side, transition time was over. Time to fish or cut bait. Get the show on the road. Etcetera, etcetera.

NO MATTER HOW BUSY WE WERE with the farm, though, my life was going to feel empty until Janilee came back. I couldn't begin to make her understand how much she'd always been a part of me and of this farm, even though she'd never set foot on it before last Saturday night. Her prior presence had been phantom, of course, a figment of a young boy's yearning daydreams. I'd thought of her so much, in so many places on the farm, that her essence must surely have permeated every building and fence post.

I'd known her since she was in the 8th grade but for a long time she didn't seem to know me from a desk bolted to the study hall floor. I was in the 10th grade when they ran out of classroom space downstairs and brought the 8th graders upstairs to the high school assembly room and I took to watching her. She was just beginning to get a sense of herself and took turns being shy and quiet and then breaking into giggles that would get her so worked up that she'd have to go get a drink of water to calm down.

Many of the teachers favored her because she was a good student, passing tests efficiently and turning in papers that were enough different from the usual run-of-the-mill junk to lift their boredom. The other girls tended to be kind of catty to her, for some reason I didn't understand, and the guys didn't know what to make of her so they sort of tuned her out.

Studious and shy myself, I pretended to ignore the entire passing scene but, by the time she was a freshman and I was in the 11th grade, she was part of my adolescent fantasy life and I had a pretty active one going. After I was old enough to drive, I would drift past her house every time I had the car to myself and thought I could do it without being noticed. Don't know what I expected to see, but even a glimpse of her mother weeding her flower garden felt like some intimate revelation about Janilee's life.

The summer after junior year was awful. I was working long hours in the fields and reading whenever there was time and sometimes I would prop a book up on the steering wheel of a piece of farm machinery. I skipped among books on the environment and detective stories. Sometimes I read old books of poetry that my Grandmother Deckard had owned and that still took up part of a shelf in the front room bookcase. I'd say some of the poems out loud to the hogs and cows while leaning on a fence post, taking care nobody who walked on two legs was within hearing distance. *Sonnets From the Portuguese* was a real turn on. I'd think about Janilee when I was in bed at night, missing seeing her, and I'd whisper, "How do I love thee? Let me count the ways..." Good thing Karl and I didn't share a room. He didn't seem to have much use for girls and he would have smacked me over the head with one of his clodhopper shoes if he'd heard me spouting poetry.

This one July afternoon I went into town to get some bags of chicken feed for Mother. As I was driving down a gravel road in the direction of our farm, I picked up a little figure in the rear mirror and realized it was Janilee on a bicycle. So I pulled over to the side and got out like I was examining my back right tire. Had to get part way into the ditch to do it, but that way I could see her. I thought I'd say, "Oh, hi!" when she rode past, as if I was surprised, and then we'd have a conversation.

She came up even with my truck and sort of looked sideways at me. "Hi!" she said, and I couldn't tell if she said it shyly or as if she hardly knew me and didn't care to.

"Hi!" I said back, so seized up with shyness that it came out strangled and lukewarm, certainly no invitation to chat.

She kept going and I went down on my knees in that ditch, watching Janilee Jasper's little ass pumping up and down on her bike while I made love to her the only way I could.

THE STUDY HALL WAS RECONFIGURED the next year and we ended up with our assigned desks pretty close. A lot of good it did me. A couple of times she asked me questions about her geometry assignment. Math was a good topic for me and I'd get so long-winded trying to answer her question thoroughly that she would lose interest and just say, "Thank you" and get out another book.

That year she met some kids from another town in some church youth group and was beginning to have what amounted to a social life, although I don't think her mother allowed her to date yet. I turned pessimistic and figured that even if I'd possibly stood a chance with her at one time, that was over. My attitude was that I'd blown three perfectly good years when we could have gotten to know one another.

I did ask her to dance at a school function or two, and was always hopeful that God or some genie would reach down to make me suave. Then, sure as anything, they'd start playing one of the new dances, which I didn't know how to do, and I'd have to make a fool of myself or make an excuse to "sit this one out." The last dances of the evening were always slow and dreamy so at the end of my senior year I thought what the heck and again asked her to dance. She accepted, with a big smile, and acted as if she was glad that I had. Not seeing any competition around, I tried to get up my nerve to ask if I could take her home but, just as I was putting the words together in my head, Karl stalked into the gym and jerked his head to get my attention. I danced Janilee over to him and he leaned forward, none too kindly, and hissed at me. There was a sick cow at the farm, he said. They hadn't been able to locate the veterinarian, and he needed my help finding him.

Refusing would be unthinkable in the Deckard culture. So I said, "Thanks," to Janilee, who hadn't heard what Karl muttered at me, and then I walked away, leaving her looking sort of bewildered. Let's just say that my social skills were about what you'd expect of a 17-year-old farm boy who hadn't been around much and who was scared of girls, anyway. I cringed over my ineptitude for months, knowing a better person than me would have found a graceful way to handle the situation.

In the fall I went on to college and when I was home there were so many farm jobs to catch up with that I hardly made it into town at all, even to get a haircut. It looked as if Dad saved stuff up for me, whenever possible, even though Karl was working on the farm full time and they also hired some extra help from time to time.

Dad kept adding farm land whenever he could but stayed mighty frugal when it came to working it. Once in a while I'd figure up how much land now belonged to us and multiply it by the going rate per acre. It didn't take a genius to figure out just how prosperous our family was but to hear Dad talk we were always headed for the poor house. I cheaped it out in school, as much as I could, making a few dollars stretch to cover room and board and books. Even so, Dad made me believe that my college education was causing financial stress at home.

What could I do except make up for lost farming time whenever I had some time?

AFTER HER GRADUATION from Ratchford High, Janilee went off to the University of Missouri on a journalism scholarship and I felt like a door had forever closed behind her. The only times I saw her after that were when she'd come back to town to visit her folks and some big town event was going on. But I'd only see her from a distance because she always had friends from college trailing after her. Later, she added a husband to her entourage but my own life had also moved on by that time. The closed door was now locked and bolted.

After her dad died and her mother remarried and moved away, Janilee didn't come back anymore. I hardly knew her married name. At class reunion dinners I sometimes asked around as to her whereabouts but nobody I talked to knew where she was or what kind of person she had turned into. She obviously had never bothered to send that information to the Ratchford alumni committee.

Dene Hellman

The first time I saw her after all those years was at the alumni reunion on Saturday night. The minute I looked at her, I could just as well have been that poor sap of a kid, down on his knees in the ditch fumbling with his pants while he watched Janilee Jasper ride down the road on her bicycle.

This time, I wasn't going to let her get away. Miracle of miracles, she felt the same way about me.

Twenty-Three

NOW, HERE I WAS, wandering the farm to collect my thoughts, sometimes sitting down for a couple of minutes in the old yard swing, then going over to the grove of trees and the creek. I moseyed along, remembering the day Janilee and I fucked our brains out in the middle of the trees and wishing she was here, now.

The water was up quite a bit due to some heavy spring rains. Karl and I would have been happy about that when we were kids. Mother tried to discourage us from wading in the creek when she wasn't there to watch, but we did anyway. Fishing wasn't particularly good but we did some of that from time to time, too.

Mostly, we'd just play. I favored cowboys and Indians but it was hard to get Karl to do that for very long. If he was really into being Big Chief and I pretended to shoot him, he'd get mad or throw himself down on the ground and bawl. He was three years older than me and should have had more control, but everybody said he was too sensitive for his own good. As he got older, he carefully concealed that part of himself but, in my opinion, just drove it inside where it festered and burned.

Generally, we collected interesting pebbles from the creek and, if we got lucky, arrowheads. We'd put the best stones in our pockets and take them back to the house where they'd end up plaguing Mother on wash day. We were always building clubhouses with fallen tree limbs. Building them was the important part because we hardly ever had any other kids over to club with. Most of our socializing took place in the country grade school we attended.

It was down the road about a mile, no walk at all for healthy kids. There were seldom any vehicles to watch out for except, at most, a slow-moving corn picker or a tractor with a manure spreader. In some parts of Iowa the country schools didn't go out of business until long after they were interesting relics in other states. A lot of the farm wives had taught country school until they got married. Our own mother was an example. At one time it was possible for a girl to go to college for a year after high school, then be eligible to teach in a one-room rural school, and that's what she had done until she and Dad were married.

Then the little one-room schoolhouses were finally voted out of business in favor of better education to be had in town. Later, the small villages began to lose out, too. The luckier towns got to keep their schools and the yellow buses would bring in kids from around the county to attend classes while the unluckier towns almost dried up and blew away without a school to anchor them. Ratchford was one of the lucky places, although it's done its share of drying up just the same. I'm still trying to make up my mind about whether general education got improved after everybody went to town school. Most everybody I went to grade school with in the little rural school had learned to read and write and spell and do arithmetic just as well as the town kids. Was it the almost one-on-one tutoring that teachers gave their pupils, or the way the older kids got assigned to help the younger ones that made up for lack of formal teacher education? Whatever, it was probably a good idea to discontinue those schools but most kids learned about as much as they wanted to, anyway, either way.

Case in point. I devoured my readers and history and geography books and was always in the back of the room marveling over the encyclopedias that were lined up on the bookshelf. Most of the time I went strictly through the alphabet, reading about Appalachian Mountains, then Bees, then Cortez. On rainy days I'd declare myself a holiday and read whatever I wanted in any of the volumes. A lot of self-discipline, a little time off for self-indulgence. It worked out pretty satisfactorily and the habit must have sunken in because it still informs the way I live.

Karl was different. He wasn't crazy about books the way I was, and he didn't always care for the teacher. He'd get sulky if he was reprimanded and since most teachers didn't want to deal with that— or with our parents, for that matter— the tendency was to leave him alone. Recess, he liked. Everybody, including the teacher, would have to play if we were going to have a softball game and he was a wonder when it was his turn at bat. He was a big kid and he could hit the ball over the fence and into Caney's cornfield if he wanted to. The other kids would try to talk him out of it because whoever was playing field would have to go after it. It usually was the little kids who had that assignment and they weren't very fast. They'd have to get down and crawl under the barbed wire and sometimes their pants would rip. Finding the ball among the cornrows wasn't simple to do, either. A whole noon recess could get eaten up that way.

Finally, when Karl was about 12, the folks decided he needed to go to school in Ratchford. For one thing, there might be some magic that would make him do better in his studies. For another thing, the 7th and 8th graders in town could play on a real ball field and he would have a chance to do more of something he was really good at.

They decided to leave me in the country school, for the time being, when Karl was enrolled in the 7th grade in town. Fine with me. I always had friends and got along with the teachers, too.

Mother took Karl to school in the mornings but it was inconvenient for her since she had to live up to a lot of Dad's expectations and normally would be out helping with chores in the morning. That would have to be fitted in with her housework and putting big meals on the table. Going to pick Karl up when school let out in the afternoons was even harder because Dad expected her to keep the books—a little chore she had to fit in before cooking supper.

Our neighbors the next farm over were the Allans. Caroline taught home economics in high school but came home every day after school let out. She must have understood what Mother was going through because she said it wouldn't be any trouble if Karl rode home with her in the afternoons. That was a big relief for Mother and she expressed her appreciation to Caroline and to Karl and me all the time.

Twenty-Four

ERNEST CAUGHT UP WITH ME mid-afternoon as I puttered in the machine shed, making one last try to get a garden tractor up and running. I hadn't felt much like communicating; too many ideas to think through, so I'd decided to mow the farmyard and the ditch between the farm frontage and the road.

"How you doing?" he asked.

From Ernest that amounted to a speech, but there was more. "Me and Marilyn would like to have you come to supper tonight," he said. "She's gonna make that meatloaf you like."

I accepted gladly. As Ernest had figured, I was primed for a long, lonely evening of missing Janilee and some companionship would be good.

Ernest and Marilyn Weist had lived in town for just about 20 years. Good people, they had sure had their share of tough luck. First, their oldest son got killed in Vietnam. Then, after they lost the farm, their middle son moved away to Lansing, taking their grandchildren with him. Their youngest son still lived in Ratchford but he was pretty slow, mentally. He had settled down the last few years to doing roofing with a Marshalltown outfit and wasn't so much of a worry anymore. Not very good company for them, but they didn't ask for miracles. His being able to support himself was blessing enough.

In the years since I'd been alone, with Karl and the folks gone, the Weists treated me like an extra son. They weren't pushy about it, but I always knew where to find a comfortable home away from home.

One winter when I had the flu so bad I could hardly hold my head up, Ernest drove me to their house, where Marilyn fixed me tomato soup made with her own home-grown and home-canned tomatoes. I had no intention of spending the night but I sort of collapsed on the daybed in their front room and the last thing I remembered before the next morning was Ernest tip-toeing over with a blanket and gently covering me up. Neither of us ever referred to that evening later, but it sat tenderly in my head. My own dad hadn't exactly been a nurturing type and I thought Ernest had probably been a better father to his sons.

ON THIS EVENING Marilyn had set a good table. We sat down and Ernest made another of his speeches. "Help yourself," he said. "Don't be bashful!" His hosting task accomplished, he sank back into his accustomed silence and let Marilyn do the talking.

Tonight I knew I owed her some details. She wasn't a gossip but she liked to know what was going on. She spent a lot of time tying World Relief quilts over at the Lutheran church with women she'd known since she was a girl so she wasn't lonely anymore like she'd been on the farm. Still, because she was very heavyset and getting more so as she aged, she couldn't get around as much as she wanted. Now, she was hoping for some tidbits that she could drop at the quilting frame as first-hand knowledge. I understood that and I wanted to oblige her a little bit.

"I hear you're engaged, Ben," she said. "Things surely can change from one week to the next! Had you been corresponding with her all this time?"

I was torn between wanting to talk and wanting to keep some things to myself. However, having an excuse to say Janilee's name out loud was a real temptation and I gave in to it.

"It's hard to explain," I said. "I guess I always had a crush on Janilee and when she came back to the reunion she was widowed, it was the right time, and it was like we picked up where we left off."

I was proud of myself for saying it like that. It made it sound like common news. Anything Janilee and I said to each other about books and the way the clouds piled up over the sunset and what made us care for one another was our own business.

"Well," said Marilyn, "I do remember that she was a smart and talented girl and I hope we'll get to be friends. How did she like her ring?"

"So Ernest does talk at home, once in a while," I thought.

The day I'd taken off, supposedly to run errands in town, I'd confided to him that I was going to Des Moines to shop for an engagement ring and that taking Janilee to dinner would be my second trip of the day to the big city.

That morning I hit all the supposedly better jewelry stores, not knowing what I was looking for but determined that Janilee's ring would make up for all the years we'd been apart. It didn't have to be super flashy but it had to be the best of whatever it was. In jewelry store terms, that meant I was going to be laying down a wad of money on it and the educated term, I found out, was *estate jewelry*.

After I settled on an heirloom emerald surrounded by what the store proprietor said were perfect diamonds, I started thinking about what I'd say to Janilee when I asked her to marry me.

Then I looked at my watch and wondered if there was enough time to make a call on a guy I'd worked with over the last two or three years. We had been together on several committees and, a year ago, I'd used my influence and a big wad of Deckard money to get him elected to one of the most important offices in Iowa. For some reason, my thoughts about him and my thoughts about Janilee's ring got mixed up together and an idea hatched. I decided to take my chances on seeing him even though I didn't have an appointment.

My dad probably rolled in his grave when I got in to see the Big Guy after only a half hour wait. Everything Dad had believed in and squeezed his nickels to acquire was just about the diametric opposite of what I believed in and spent my own nickels to make happen.

If this Iowa politician had been in office in Dad's day, Dad would have wanted to stick pins in an effigy to destroy him. Maybe he would have succeeded. There were and still are plenty of people around who are fine farmers according to traditional beliefs but shortsighted in the long run. At least, I sometimes thought to myself, Dad would approve that I had no interest in personally running for office, even when urged to do so. My personal plans were as elaborate as any politician's but more along the line of hard work than backing up my agenda with charismatic handshakes.

However, the charismatic handshakes are needed and, when Himself bounded into the reception area to greet me, I thought how important he could be if his career expanded to a national level. He believed, as much as I did, in doing something about conservation and world hunger and global warming. We just had different ways of going about it. He knew a lot about agriculture because he came from a long line of prosperous Iowa farmers but his expertise lay in communication whereas I was a hands-on farmer.

"Hey, Ben!" he roared, grabbing my shoulder with one hand and shaking my hand with the other. "What brings you in today?"

He was big—very big.

I probably measure six feet, with a hefty chest and pretty well toned biceps, thanks to a lifetime of outdoor work. He might top out at 6'6", and was as well set up as a dedicated gym regimen could make him. Few people, friend or enemy, would take him for granted.

His A-one personality, together with a finely honed intellect, labeled him "WINNER" wherever he went. And, I ruefully had to acknowledge, he hadn't yet turned forty so had plenty of time to meet his own expectations. This seventh generation Iowan was the absolute epitome of the fictitious native son that Janilee and I had joked about earlier in the week.

"I'm looking to get engaged and married," I told him. "I'm marrying somebody I've been in love with most of my life. She's from out of state, but is moving back. She doesn't know it yet, but she'll be an incredible asset. Her training and work is in communications and, independently, she's spent the last several years rescuing endangered plants. How's that for an ideal match?"

More shoulder gripping and some slaps on the back. Charisma aside, this guy was genuinely happy for me. He also figured out that I wasn't paying him a mid-day visit just to bring him my news.

"How can I be of help?" he asked.

"For today," I said, "you can assume the alias *Ivan Schroder* and be at the Marquis restaurant to give Janilee her ring. She doesn't know Iowa VIPs from Adam and Eve."

I told him the native son story that Janilee and I had cooked up in the Ratchford café and he bent over double laughing. I'd figured that would be his reaction. He'd like playing the Ivan role just for the hell of it and, additionally, a little piece of him would make a chalk mark in the part of his brain that records favors owed, favors repaid, and favors once again owed.

I handed over the fancy box with Janilee's ring.

"See you tonight!" I said as I walked out the door.

Sure enough, that evening he followed through like a Hollywood pro and damn near swept Janilee off her feet.

Twenty-Five

KNOWING HOW MUCH MARILYN WEIST would enjoy being in on a secret, I decided to tell her some of that story.

"Janilee still doesn't quite remember how to take Iowans," I said. "She doesn't realize that we're changing some of our ways and she made up this stereotype of somebody she imagined Iowans would want to see as president of the United States. She called him 'Ivan Schroeder.' Well, after I found the ring I wanted, I went over to Big Guy's office. He knew me pretty well from committees we'd worked on together so I got in to see him right away.

"We hatched a scheme where he'd be in the same place we were that evening and he'd walk over and introduce himself to Janilee as 'Ivan Schroder' and hand her the ring.

"She doesn't know who's who around here and she was pretty taken aback when that happened. She really didn't have a clue. We never got around to talking about it later, so eventually I'll have the fun of introducing them for real. His name might not be 'Ivan' but who knows? She may someday have the pleasure of dancing at his inaugural ball, anyhow!"

Marilyn loved that story and promised to keep it quiet. As a follow-up reward, I told her about the plan to build a new environmentally with-it farmhouse. That was news to Ernest, too, and he looked like he had questions about how so many changes might affect him.

Two or three years ago I'd taken care of his and Marilyn's old age, without telling them about it. Not that I expected to pass on before they did but I had no heirs and the Weists felt like family. My lawyer talked me into putting my affairs in order so I'd had him draw up a will just in case. I divided whatever estate there might be among a bunch of causes that I favored, including the well-being of Ernest and Marilyn. Some of that would have to be readjusted after Janilee and I were married, but there would always be a generous allowance for the Weists even if I wasn't around to see to it.

For now, I needed Ernest more than ever and this was a good time to tell him. "Life is going to be different after Janilee comes back to stay," I said. "There's the house to build, and a lot more activity coming up for me on the state level. The time has come to take my seed bank and livestock diversification projects to a higher level. Also, it's time to get out and do a little socializing around the area so she'll feel at home."

Ernest and Marilyn looked worried. Change had rarely been a good thing in their lives.

I continued. "I'm still going to handle the business end of things, but I won't have time to be tied down with day-to-day farm needs. Ernest, we're going to need more help, year round, not just seasonally the way it has been. I'm putting you in charge of all that and you need to hire some steady, knowledgeable guys who know their way around a farm and aren't afraid of new ideas. I'll raise your wages to management level and tomorrow morning we need to decide what we have to pay to get dependable people and what we'll expect of them.

Marilyn looked relieved and pleased and Ernest nodded as if he'd known it all along. I said goodnight and drove home thinking what good people they are and how lucky I was to have this new lease on life.

I DIDN'T CONSIDER MYSELF anything special, but what Janilee and I had found together, now that we were reunited, was beyond special. In my experience and to my knowledge, such a close feeling doesn't happen to many couples. Lots of them get along okay and have an average happy married life, but not the kind of bond we'd both felt right away. I'll admit that I was doing some heavy daydreaming, even including in the picture those two sons of hers who were environmental experts, both by inclination and education. Maybe the Deckard farm had a future in the next generation, after all.

It was still light when I got back to the farm from the Weists and I didn't want to go inside just yet, so I began walking around, thinking where the new house would go. Because we'd have to live in the old house while building was going on, it meant the new one would need to be sited farther back from the road and closer to the old orchard.

I took my foot and bunched the grass leavings from the afternoon mowing into little ridges to outline the walls. Pretty soon, I found myself sitting down in the middle of the "walls," daydreaming about Janilee and what it would be like to have a wife and new house. I might be facing middle age, but I had no experience with living the kind of regular household life eventually experienced by most rural adults.

95

To begin with, when Karl and I were growing up on the farm, what the folks told us to do and not do was the same as it was in most farm families only more so. As long as our feet were under their table at mealtimes, it couldn't be said independent thinking was encouraged. Karl would paste a sulky look on his face when he felt thwarted while I would just think my own thoughts, but we never mouthed off.

We weren't poor. Dad had inherited the place and so had his father before him. Like Mother, he had a little bit of college education and he was a good, conservative businessman who pinched pennies somewhat beyond common discretion. He was the kind of alpha male who thought he naturally knew best about everything and convinced Mother of that during all of their married life.

Dad's thrift got in the way of his family's happiness at times—even Mother's. When the old farmhouse got too rickety for comfort, Mother wanted to replace it with one of those one-story ranch houses like the Allens had. Dad would have none of it and hired carpenters to strengthen and redo whatever was called for on the old house. The closest thing Mother got to a ranch house was an ugly picture window that put us all on view in the evening when the lights were on—unless an equally ugly set of curtains was drawn.

By the time the bathroom was up for remodeling, Mother was getting stubborn. She wanted a pink one and Dad was horrified. "What kind of color is that for a farm?" he asked.

Mother threw one of the only prima donna fits of her life, yelling and sobbing until Dad couldn't handle it. He backed down and let her have pink. He also had the plumbers install a shower and toilet down in the basement and, from then on, that's all he used. When he got older and the prostate problems kicked in and he started having to get up at all hours of the night, he must have stood in front of the pink toilet with his eyes shut so he wouldn't have to acknowledge the folly of backing down.

By high school, Karl got so he'd just use the facilities in the basement, too. Mother was kind of embarrassed by then. She saw a picture in a home decorating magazine where somebody cut the effect of a pink bathroom, supposedly making it sophisticated, by accessorizing with bright red towels. She got some and hung them up.

Personally, I thought the whole thing was funny as hell and only got bothered when one of the red towels would get into the wrong load of laundry and Dad and Karl and I would end up with a stack of pink underwear that wouldn't wash white for weeks.

Twenty-Six

AFTER HIGH SCHOOL I went on to college and dorm rooms. Not being overly neat, myself, it wasn't traumatic if I got a slob for a roommate. Home base during the school years was not a cozy retreat, to my way of thinking, just a place to change clothes and sleep. And summers were spent helping out on the farm.

Then I graduated, got drafted, and ended up at a desk out in Wyoming looking at blueprints for airbases. There, I shared an off-base apartment with a couple of other guys. One of them was particular about things and sort of kept house but I wasn't tuned in to how it looked as long as I had a place to sleep and, once in a while, bring a girl home.

When I got out of the Service, I went back to college for a Master's. Life was casual on campus. Even some strictly brought up young women were lying around on mattresses on the floor puffing weed and acting out the sexual revolution. The scene was exciting to all of us rural guys who had been hand-raised by traditional parents. Unlike our parents' generation, having a house with a yard and a garage was the last thing most of us wanted. Hanging on at school, on the other hand, was a seductive lifestyle, even for a studious person like me.

About the time my G.I. Bill was running out, I got serious. The environment was still my first love, the big decision being whether I'd opt for a career with the Iowa Department of Natural Resources or the Army Corps of Engineers. I took a temporary job as an instructor in the college science department and that's when I met Cordelia, who was scoping out classes taught by eligible bachelors. She was a second grade teacher in a local school and had already picked out her silverware and china patterns.

Cordelia wanted to get married. It was what she studied on, every day, after her regular lesson plans were finished. She even had a scrapbook that she pasted full of recipes and magazine articles about furniture styles.

By this time, I was fairly sick of the free-and-easy scene and getting married seemed consistent with my career hopes. Cordelia was cute and liked to cook and, besides, Mother said she was "ladylike." Whenever Cordelia and I went out to the farm for Sunday dinner, Mother would get out Grandmother Deckard's linen napkins and look in the back of her Betty Crocker cookbook to see where the dessert spoon should go. One Sunday she even asked Caroline and Harold Allan over to dinner. Caroline and Cordelia had a wonderful time comparing notes on lady things, while Mother smiled shyly in the background. I don't think she was ever totally comfortable with her future daughter-in-law but she never uttered a word of complaint to me, then or later.

Down the aisle we went and it seemed to work out okay. Whatever Cordelia wanted was the way it was, even when I found some of our domestic life tedious. I wished that I had the guts to say so, not that Cordelia would have taken kindly to changing lanes, but we never did seem to find much of mutual interest to talk about. Our first home was a shabby apartment in the upstairs of a professor's house but we looked forward to my potential career as an environmentalist. Actually, I looked forward to being an environmentalist and Cordelia happily anticipated staying at home to have kids and entertain important guests. Convinced that I would have a successful career, she had dreams of living out in the state of Washington or, maybe, someplace in Arizona. She added pictures of patios with seascape views and Southwestern Mission-style houses to her scrapbook.

Then Dad came to see me. "Karl is going through some bad times," he said. "He isn't able to handle the farm and I can't find anybody trustworthy to take over. Things aren't going so well for me, health-wise, so I can't even depend on myself. You better come back to the farm and manage things until we get on our feet."

The immediate path was clear cut for me. My folks had never placed any unacceptable demands on me, always encouraging me, once I grew up, to move forward with my own plans as long as I supported myself. Now, they needed to keep the farm and themselves solvent. Cordelia and I would have to move home to the Ratchford farm, at least for now.

Only Cordelia wasn't about to stand for it. "I'm not cut out to be a farmer's wife," she said. "They could get along just fine if they wanted to; they have the money to hire all kinds of help. You have a choice even if you don't think so. The farm or me."

It was not an option I could handle. While I wanted to take on the promise and challenge of my chosen career, I couldn't turn my back when my family needed me.

Additionally—perhaps most importantly—an artificial haze lay over life with Cordelia. In two years, it hadn't lifted and she and our life together failed to integrate, no matter how many scrapbooks she pasted up.

I said, "Cordelia, for better or worse you married a farmer. Going back home to help out is what I need to do."

Our parting was amiable enough. We were no worse off than dozens of couples around campus who had simply been shacking up without benefit of clergy and most of whom broke up when a little maturity set in.

She offered me half the wedding presents. Not having any particular interest in eight place settings of Franciscan china or a bunch of pickle forks, I said "No thanks," and moved back into my old room at the farm. Cordelia undoubtedly moved on the next year and had a nice start to her hope chest. I'm ashamed to say I was never interested enough or bored enough to find out.

I had my hands full with keeping the farm going, helping Mother take care of Dad and easing things for her as, first, Dad died and then, after a while, Karl died.

Twenty-Seven

LATER, THERE WERE A FEW GIRLFRIENDS, nothing serious, nobody I'd want to set up housekeeping with. Farming got to be a deep satisfaction as my methods transitioned from the agricultural routines of Dad's generation toward more organic techniques. It didn't endear me to area farmers but later, when they saw my compromises continue to bring in good money, most of them went back to friendly neighborliness.

In the last year and a half, my casual attitude toward women changed a little bit when Marlys Gauch came to work in the Ratchford Bank. She was a tall, nice-looking woman who right away took an interest in community life. She sang in the Congregational church choir and helped plan outings for the old folks at the Ratchford Nursing Home. I asked her out shortly after I met her at a bank board meeting, and had a suspicion that she and the whole town soon took it for granted that we were a match.

God knows she tried hard enough, working all angles from home-cooked meals to whatever was possible to keep things lively in bed. She had an apartment downtown and once, when we were getting into my truck to go someplace, she felt chilly and asked me to go back upstairs to get a jacket out of her bedroom closet.

As I took it off its hanger, I noticed a stack of *Cosmopolitan* magazines on the closet floor. Since I'm always curious about people's reading material, I bent down to take a look and got flustered because every one of them had a cover title like "Enhance your sex life with these three techniques!" or "Two things he wishes you'd do to him!"

While I wasn't above enjoying whatever Marlys thought up, it was somehow disconcerting to think I'd been entertained cook-book recipe style. Closing the closet door quickly, I could feel my face was red when I gave Marlys her jacket.

Still, it was kind of stimulating to round a field on my tractor on the afternoon of date nights, wondering if she had a new Cosmo issue and was memorizing five more ways to turn me on.

Several months ago, I began giving thought to proposing to Marlys. There might be advantages to this, in addition to feeling more settled and less chronically horny. She had a good business head on her shoulders, which would be a decided asset, and although she was no Cordelia about household things, she would represent a social advantage. That was my head talking, not my heart.

One evening I dressed extra carefully, thinking maybe this was a good time to broach the subject of a fall wedding. I even went against my usual dislike of men's cologne, took out a bottle of it that somebody had given me a year or so before, unscrewed the cap and sniffed. Not so bad, after all. I don't know what got into me then. I put a couple of dabs where I thought it would do the most good, in the general vicinity of my pelvis.

Marlys maybe sensed that I was getting close to decision time because she pulled out all the stops from the minutes I walked in her door. The way she acted, I figured she had two or three sets of Cosmo magazine ideas going at once. It was going to be some night. Right after a knockout meal, Marlys started off by coaxing me back to her bedroom and announcing her intention to kiss me all over. Knowing I'd make it up to her big time, later, I laid back to let it happen.

As Marlys headed south, she started choking up. That choking worked up to gasping, then into some audible version of asphyxiation.

I rolled off the bed and Marlys took off for the bathroom where she evidently kept an inhaler and some kind of allergy medicine. Between heaving pants, she let me know she was going to live but that whatever scent I was wearing had triggered a Class A reaction and I was not to come near.

As soon as I knew she was all right, I put on my pants and left. I sat on a curb down on Main Street for some time, feeling like a fool, listening to a squadron of bugs dive-bomb the street lights, before I felt collected enough to drive home.

After that, it seemed like Marlys' allergies got in the way of whatever I tried to plan. I'd taken a wait-and-see attitude, postponing the idea about getting married, but she started pushing on me with some not-so-subtle hints. Like Cordelia before her, she appeared to have some sort of personal agenda that might or might not work well for me.

She had another allergy attack when I brought her out to the farmhouse and explained to me afterward that old houses have molds that linger. The obvious solution, I figured, would be a new house but that didn't bother me. There was a lot of money piling up in the

Ratchford bank that was mine to use or not use any way I chose.

Another time, I brought her out to the farm and we skipped the house but then she choked up just walking around the barnyard. It was beyond me how we could have a life together unless we lived in town and I drove out to the country every morning, a thought I hated but that she seemed to be promoting in a subtle, hinting way.

THAT'S WHERE I WAS with my thinking up to the time of the high school reunion, seeing Janilee again, and knowing right away that I wanted her in my life. I'd carried a faint outline of the woman she was in my head for years and years, without any expectation such a person would ever materialize. Cordelia and Marlys didn't come close.

Marlys and I had a date scheduled for the weekend after the reunion. When Janilee and I went into town on Tuesday, I walked into the Ratchford Bank and found Marlys behind the teller's window.

"I'm sorry, Marlys," I said. "I have to cancel this next weekend's plans."

She just looked at me sadly and nodded. News travels fast in Ratchford and she obviously had heard about Janilee and me taking up with one another on Saturday night and being inseparable since. I felt kind of bad about disappointing Marlys but also thought with all her Cosmo magazine strategies, she would land some prosperous rural widower in no time at all. One who didn't live on a farm and who stayed away from Eau de Chanel for Men.

All in all, before Janilee there had never, in the last 20 years, been a right time or woman to make me eager for commitment. Now, all I wanted was for her to hurry back to me.

Twenty-Eight

IT WAS DARK BY NOW and the fireflies were beginning to wink on and off. I stood up from my grassy blueprint in the backyard and went inside, where I opened a window the better to hear the night noises. Sitting down at my computer, I typed in "Midwestern architects who specialize in green architecture."

As the names spilled out, a peripheral sadness came along with these joyous visions of the future. When this old house tumbled in on itself and was deliberately buried under 20 feet of prairie topsoil, I feared its history would call out to me repeatedly, right up through the ground. As Janilee and I designed gardens and worked in them, when her future grandchildren romped in the spacious farmyard, would I pick up reproachful echoes of all the generations that had gone before us? This guilt at destroying the family home would be cargo I would have to carry alone. No one, least of all Janilee, should have to share it with me.

Many of my people had quietly lived their lives here, of course, and the ratio of good times to bad ones, over 150 years, was beyond my guess. A lot of them were buried in the Ratchford cemetery and I'd always meant to talk to some of the town's oldsters to find out more about family history. Now it was too late to ever learn their stories and I regretted it. I had been busy with my own concerns during the years when Mother and Dad and my aunt would have gladly told me all I wanted to know. Now, it was time to move on. However, I was certain of one thing: few tales from the past could compare with the tragedy represented by my brother, Karl.

CLIMBING THE STAIRS, I went past the room where I had slept for most of my life and into Karl's old room. There probably hadn't been 10 nights out of his short life when he hadn't been here and there hadn't been many times after his death when I had opened the door to his room. I looked up at his gruesome poster collection that papered almost the entire wall and understood Janilee's dismay when she laid out her number one priority upon her return.

"As soon as I get back," she had said, "we have to clear out that room. Before we do one other thing! It gives me the shivers. We're going to be living in the old house for as long as it takes to build the new one and I don't want to think about the monsters simmering away behind that closed door every time I go upstairs."

Mother had been upset by Karl's collection, as well, but she put everything into her own choice of perspective.

"He was such a sweet little boy," she frequently said.

Well, no, he wasn't, but if Mother wanted to remember him that way it was okay with me.

What he was, in my memory, was sullen, with his feelings hurt too easily for comfortable co-existence even after we got past our early childhood years. Three years older than me, he was always bigger and better looking—a situation that continued to hold true into our adulthood. It never bothered me because I got ego gratification from being a better student, as well as from my ability to adapt to life as it played out around me. I took it as a compliment when someone described me as "laid back."

Since I was a low-maintenance child, according to Mother, a lot of her day-to-day child-rearing efforts centered around Karl. If he pouted, she was uneasy as to the cause. If he was on the verge of tears, she was quick to suggest a happy idea. As I played contentedly on the floor with toys Karl had quickly rejected when they were his, Mother would pull him onto her lap, smooth out the frown lines between his eyes, and praise him for some reason only she could contrive.

After the folks took him out of country school and enrolled him in town, Karl had a chance to use his gift for athletics on the Ratchford ball field. In a way, he acted happier than we had ever seen him. But, after a while, he would no longer allow Mother to touch him, jerking away if she so much as went to smooth his shirt collar.

"Let him be!" was Dad's assessment when Mother worried about that. "What do you expect of a guy? He's no sissy and he'll get touchy-feely again when he's old enough to have a girlfriend!"

As the 7th and 8th grades passed and 14-year-old Karl went into high school, his moroseness grew. He did his chores at home, he had passing grades at school, but his only visible pleasure was confined to moments on the ball field.

He gave up all pretense of interacting with me. Since I usually preferred using my coveted spare time to read a book, rather than in pitching or batting, bonding time ceased. Once in a while, he and Dad would smack a few balls across the road and into the pasture but Dad seldom took the time off. If we didn't handle all the farm work, it would mean getting a hired man—and Dad was much too tight-fisted to court that expense.

Twice, during those years, I woke up in the middle of the night to find Karl in my room, leaning over my bed. He acted as if he wanted to tell me something, or maybe ask me something, but he'd back off and go on out of the room without saying anything at all. I'd pretend to be sleeping when that happened and the next day would feel guilty about not trying to talk to him.

Mother got increasingly worried. Looking back, I can understand that having a child, doing the best one knows to do for that child, idealizing that child, then seeing the child turn into a stranger, must belong to a unique and terrible set of sorrows. At the time, I was merely a mute bystander—not exactly insensitive but inept for sure.

She eventually decided on her own, without consulting Dad, to go to school and see if Karl's teachers had insights that their teaching education had surely provided. Years later, she told me that she had singled out Mr. Door, the school superintendent, because he was the boys' athletic coach. Of all the faculty, Earl Door probably was the best advisor she could have chosen.

Mr. Door was a godsend to Ratchford School. Kind, considerate, intelligent, he cared about the needs of all the kids and showed it in ways that few others would. It turned out that he, also, was concerned about Karl. After making Mother radiantly happy by raving about Karl's promising athletic talents and the choices this would open to him, he voiced some apprehensions.

"Karl doesn't open up to anybody," he said. "He withdraws from all of us; doesn't even want to shower with the other guys. Sometimes, I wish he'd do something really mischievous so I'd have an excuse to sit him down for a man-to-man talk."

"What should I do?" Mother asked.

"This goes beyond normal teen-age behavior," said Mr Door. "My advice would be to take him over to Des Moines or to Iowa City and let him visit with a specialist in adolescent psychology. I'll be glad to get some references together, if you like."

Mother went home thoughtfully and broached the subject to Dad, who promptly hit the ceiling.

"Nothing wrong with him!" he raged. "His Grandfather Deckard was no talker, either. Didn't stop him from being the best farmer in the county! And Grandmother Deckard doted on him through 55 years of married life, so he knew how to keep a woman happy, too!"

Mother backed down, but she did ask a couple more people for an opinion. The Congregational preacher waved away her concerns and said he wished every kid in his Sunday school class was as well behaved and as interested in Old Testament bible stories as Karl Deckard. And Caroline Allan said Karl was the most courteous, sweet and accommodating young man she had ever known.

Mother handily went into denial.

Karl turned 16 about the time I finished 8th grade in the country school and entered Ratchford High. Since there were two of us going into town every day, Dad got us an old Ford beater for our transportation needs. Karl no longer had to hitch rides home with Caroline Allan and he appeared to perk up, some, with his new responsibility to deliver himself and me to school safely and on time.

He lived for baseball season. He never looked as free as he did when he'd batted a ball farther than anybody could reasonably expect and was running the bases like he had wings on his feet. Mother and I always went to his home games and upon occasion Dad would go, too. Too proud to clap and holler for his own boy, he would just sit there with a broad, proud grin on his face whenever Karl did something noticeable.

By now, Karl was well over six feet tall, had massive shoulders, a shock of dark hair, and was a pleasure to look at. I'd see girls' stares slide right past me and settle on him. Maybe, in a way, he favored Dad and his side of the family while I took after Mother's folks a little bit.

Outside of farm work, the one thing that we three Deckard men did together was head into town a couple of Saturday nights a month to have Harry Ansel, the local barber, cut our hair. When Harry cut Karl's, he'd always say, "Now I've been barbering for 30 years and one thing I do appreciate is a good head of hair. Karl, you've got one of the best. You take care of it, now!"

Karl never acknowledged the compliment, but his hair did seem to be his one vanity and he kept it well combed. As a good athlete, he got by with the other guys despite his silent ways. He didn't respond to the girls twittering over him and never gave a sign of picking out one of them as a favorite, which probably disappointed the more ambitious mothers who had an eye out for Deckard money.

Then he graduated from high school and helped Dad on the farm full time. As soon as he could get by with it, he stopped going to church on Sundays with Mother, Dad and me. Twice a month he still went with us to get his hair cut, and he played on a Ratchford men's ball team in decent weather. That was the extent of his social life.

Three years after him, I graduated and went on to college. Ames wasn't far, so I was home pretty often to help out in the fields. It causes shame when I recall that during my first four years at Ames and then my two flightless years in the Air Force, I hardly gave Karl a thought unless I was at the farm. He'd be there, always quiet to the point of being hostile, his few words having to do with work.

In a way, Dad accepted Karl's ways, but I suppose he would have enjoyed a little more companionship as the two of them toiled side by side—especially when his health began to go downhill. Even the closemouthed have things they want or need to say, from time to time. Maybe true for Dad, but not for Karl.

Mother never complained about being lonely but seemed extraordinarily happy to have me come home on weekends and sometimes she would talk my head off. She was a quiet lady, essentially, but if I lingered at the table a bit longer than Dad and Karl, she would shoot such a stream of words at me that I'd lose track of the topic. While I was willing to listen, it was hard going when Mother would ease up and expect me to give her all kinds of details about my life on the campus. Outside of studying hard, very little of what I did made appropriate stories for a mother's ears. I wasn't misbehaved by most current standards, but times were changing and I found many of the changes interesting and pleasurable. Mother would have interpreted them as more reasons to worry and I didn't want her to do any more worrying than she already was.

Twenty-Nine

DURING THE FOUR YEARS after my Air Force interlude, as I plodded away at advanced degrees, explored the attitudes of lately liberated women, then courted and married Cordelia, it seemed to me that Karl began to loosen up and take more interest in things.

It puzzled me that he never had a girlfriend, or even sought the acquaintance of women. My own hormones had been jiggling since I was a young teenager so I wondered if, despite his masculine appearance, he was low on testosterone or, possibly, gay. Dad and Mother might have had the same thoughts but, if they did, they kept it from me.

The first time I brought Cordelia to the farm for Sunday dinner, Karl looked at us with a glimmer of interest. However, it was the sort of interested look you'd give to seeing the local banker lead a monkey on a string. Cordelia was determined to make a favorable impression on everyone and was successful as far as the folks were concerned. I hadn't prepared her for Karl, except to say he was single, lived at home, and was "quiet."

After he gifted her with a lukewarm handshake, she decided to go the direct question route.

Cordelia: "How long have you been farming, Karl?"

Karl: "Always."

Cordelia: "What do you do for fun?"

Karl: "Baseball."

Cordelia: "I have a girlfriend I'd just love to have you meet. Are you interested?"

Karl: "No."

She gave up. On our way back home she queried me for a while, then retreated when my answers were almost as monosyllabic as Karl's. "But he's so good looking!" she exclaimed, as if that was of significant importance.

On ensuing visits, she did what the rest of us did, assuming Karl's presence at the dinner table was as far as he was going to go toward sociability. Sometimes Mother demanded, with one of those "Mother looks" that are capable of icing up the blood of their children, no matter how old they are, that he linger for a while longer. He would then sit there, arms folded across his chest, until

109

she got so uncomfortable that she'd excuse him with a nod.

But he did start playing his radio once in a while and Mother told me that occasionally, if he happened to be in the house, he'd watch the evening news if Dad had it turned on.

Instead of steadily improving, though, he slid into depression. It was almost as if he had become more responsive to the world only to discover that he was badly out of tune with it. His hair got shaggy because he stopped going regularly into town with Dad for haircuts. He would probably have grown a beard, out of plain old neglect, if Dad had stood for it.

There were days, few at first but then more frequent, when he wouldn't leave his bed. Mother would go in his room and ask, "Are you sick? Can I do anything for you?" and he would shake his head "no" and turn his face to the wall. By the next morning, he'd be up and out doing chores. Mother decided he had some pains and aches he didn't want to disclose because he knew she had her hands full with Dad's health problems. The folks were going back and forth to the Mayo Clinic in Minnesota by then, and needed him to be responsible for the farm.

One Friday they got home from one of those trips to Rochester to find the cattle bawling in the pen closest to the house. The animals obviously hadn't been fed for at least a day, maybe longer.

The next week was when Dad came to Ames and asked me to come back to the farm and take over, for a while, until everyone was healthy and back on their feet..

After I moved back, I could see Karl begin to ease up, becoming less grim, more able to get up and face the day. He still didn't get his hair cut but he pulled it back with an old rubber band, even tucked it under his cap on the rare times he had to go into Ratchford.

DAD STRUGGLED with his renal problems. Or, rather, Mother struggled with Dad's renal disease. He had largely given up; if he couldn't be out running things on the farm, he didn't care about much else. I helped in every way I could and so did Karl, who went out of his way to deal with the hospital equipment and get Dad's personal needs taken care of.

By the time Dad passed away, Karl was into religion. It started with his radio being tuned to the evangelistic preachers who ranted and raved around the clock. I couldn't make out what they were saying and didn't want to. My assumption was that Karl was taking

Dad's lingering death hard and found comfort in their preaching, but their tone of voice didn't strike me as soothing. In fact, it irritated me and if I hadn't wanted to avoid distressing Mother, I would have yelled, "Turn down that shit before I turn it down for you!" "Laid back" only goes so far when propaganda is the order of the day.

A couple of months after Dad's funeral, Karl started going into Des Moines on Sundays to some kind of church he heard about on the radio. He didn't say what it was and I sure didn't ask.

Then he began ordering those damn posters. They came in tubes that barely fit into the mailbox, two and three a month, from some Kansas City address. Between the collection plate at his church and the poster orders, he must have spent more money, as soon as he had some, than he had in a decade. I hadn't been aware that Dad had stopped paying him years before, but wasn't surprised when I examined the books and saw no pay going to Karl or any tax records for him. Between Dad's thriftiness and Karl's lack of interest in the outside world, it was just more money left in the Deckard account at the Ratchford Bank. Dad had probably figured that Karl would get his due in time.

Certainly, I had no intention of having empty pockets and, since I was now keeping the books, I paid Karl, too. While I cringed at the thought of hard-earned money going to support those radio programs Karl listened to, it was his privilege to be a contributor to whatever he wanted.

I hardly ever looked into his room even then but, when I did, I was disgusted at the new art work. How anybody could associate those ugly things with religion was beyond me. Anyway, my hands were full and I tried not to think too much. Leaving my Doctorate unfinished was harder than parting from Cordelia. On some level, I knew I wasn't ever going to get back to academia and the career path I'd chosen. It was one day at a time for now.

Karl took to preaching at me, and sometimes at Mother. For a while, it was a relief for us to hear that he still knew how to string sentences together. Then we wished he'd shut up and turn silent again.

"The wages of sin are death!" he'd say, then repeat the words of the radio preachers for a half hour at a time. Mother got to the point where she'd fix dinner for us, then go on into Ratchford to visit her sister for the rest of the afternoon.

Looking for an excuse of my own, I started buying books when I went into Des Moines and read them at the table. When Karl interrupted me with one of his rants I'd ignore him until he was quiet, then go back outside to work. There was plenty of that, since Karl slacked off again. He didn't take to his bed any more, but he could be just as useless. After Ernest Weist's farm went under, I went into town and asked him if he'd come work for us. It was a huge relief when he said yes and brought a degree of sanity to the farm with him.

There was a really bad day that fall, around harvest time. It had rained off and on since early morning, big fat thunder boomers, complete with lightning zigzagging across the sky. Between afternoon storms, I was heading toward the barn when the hay mow door flew open and I saw Karl up there. His cap was off and about a year of wild, uncut hair was streaming around his face. He was screaming, a hayseed Savanarola.

"Fear God and give glory to him…for the hour of his judgment is come…Babylon is fallen, is fallen…because she made all nations drink of the wine of the wrath of her fornication…If any man worship the beast and his image…the same shall drink of the wine of the wrath of God…and he shall be tormented with fire and brimstone…and the smoke of their torment ascendeth up for ever and ever…and they have no rest day nor night who worship the beast and his image…"

How long he would go on like that, I wondered. Should I let him wear himself out? Should I go up in the hay mow and try to reason with him? The way he was teetering around on the edge of the open door scared me so I didn't want to make any sudden moves.

Ernest, who had been out of sight around the corner of the barn, listening, came around to the front then. Standing under the hay mow door, he looked up and said, as calmly as you please, "Karl, can you give me a hand? It's going to pour rain again, any minute now, and those feed sacks need to be moved into the shed."

Once a farmer, always a farmer. Karl glowered down at him a minute, then he turned around, climbed down out of the barn loft, and began helping Ernest move the bags.

Thirty

AFTER THAT, KARL BEGAN improving again. Several times we had thought so, only to be disappointed as he went into another phase that was just as difficult as the last but this time was somehow different. I had to give Ernest credit for the slow transformation. Not a talker himself, he had no communication goals for Karl. Instead, he had a nice, easy way about him that must have been a change from Dad's stern, sometimes irritable ways. I don't think I had been guilty of irritability with Karl but I had, by default, become the brother who was in charge and that had to be aggravating to a sibling.

It is my thought that Ernest gradually became a gentle father figure because sometimes Karl gave the impression of following him around. In turn, Ernest treated him like a co-worker of merit, even deferring to him at times as if to an employer, one of the Deckards, after all. Sometimes I'd muse to myself whether Ernest was deliberately being therapeutic or if he just did what came naturally. Ernest being Ernest, that was something I'd never find out.

Karl still took off for Sunday church meetings in Des Moines, but he slowly cut down on the radio preachers. Instead, in off-hours he began to sit at the old desk in his room, writing. I never saw what he wrote but noticed that he went into town to the post office a couple of times a week.

My assumption was that he still ordered posters or, maybe, still sent money to evangelists he liked. I was surprised when letters began showing up in our rural mailbox addressed to him. When I picked up the mail, or when Mother had done so and left it on the kitchen table, I couldn't help but notice that the envelopes were in Karl's handwriting, addressed to himself. Why anyone would go to the trouble of writing a letter, putting a stamp on it and going to town to mail it if it was just going to be delivered right back to him, was an enigma. But Karl had been an oddball for so long that it was useless to waste time reasoning.

Entering the kitchen one day, just in time to see me looking over the day's mail, he asked a peculiar question. "Is it true that if you want to prove something you write it out, mail it to yourself, and then keep the postmarked envelope unopened?"

I said I'd heard that, too, but didn't know for sure. Thinking it over later, I thought perhaps Karl had made a donation to somebody and wanted proof for his income tax.

OVER THE NEXT YEAR OR SO, he improved so much that he actually started taking some initiative. Once in a while, he would volunteer a casual remark to Mother and, when she asked him once if he might go back to playing on the Ratchford men's baseball team, he said he was thinking about it. His hair was down-his-back long by now. It didn't bother me but it distressed Mother. I had a notion to ask Ernest if he'd suggest to Karl some Saturday that they knock off work and go get haircuts.

Then the worst happened. Of course, it had to be on an early spring day when Mother was in Ratchford at her sister's house, Ernest was out in the farthest field and I was in Ames attending a farm business seminar.

As we reconstructed it, Karl had taken it into his head to inject some of the heifers. It wasn't particularly a job for the vet; for one reason or another, some farms kept a supply of animal antibiotic on hand, along with disposable syringes. Care had to be taken when doing this chore, but there was little history of accidents. Farmers who raised cattle knew the ropes.

Evidently, Karl had a heifer in the barn in a squeeze chute. He had filled a syringe with enough antibiotic to do the job and was holding it when something startled him and he fell, jabbing himself with the needle, piercing his coveralls and shooting the stuff into his groin. The right amount for an 800 pound cow is enough to kill even a big, strong man—and that's what happened.

Ernest found him when he came in from the field and it was too late, even if the antibiotic had had an antidote, which it didn't. Karl was gone long before Ernest found him, certainly before emergency responders arrived. There was a brief investigation, but so many freak farm accidents happen all the time that rural people have a certain amount of fatalism in their outlook.

There was nothing left to do except plan the funeral. Harry Ansel, who was mostly retired by now, went over to the funeral home and cut Karl's hair. Mother insisted on a visitation evening and everybody, even the folks who had for years pointed Karl out as "strange," talked about how handsome he was and what a shame he'd had the accident. Sympathy cards filled our mailbox and the folks we knew acted as if there hadn't ever been anything unusual about Karl.

Stunned at this second death in her family, Mother gave up. Apologizing profusely to me for what she considered abandonment, she gave the farmhouse one last cleaning, filled up the freezer with enough baked goods and casseroles to feed an army, and moved into her sister's house in town. I think she meant to come out to the farm and do things for me every few weeks but, once she got into town she took to going out to the Ratchford cemetery every day to visit Dad's and Karl's graves. After a couple of years, it seemed like she felt so sad that she just wanted to move in with them and then she was gone and I had the final date carved on the double tombstone she shared with Dad.

Thirty-One

ALL THAT WAS BEHIND ME NOW. The past several years had allowed plenty of time to read, reflect, recover my social inclinations, and take my pick of worthy causes to pursue. The pros and cons of environmental issues kept farmers polarized, often along political lines, and could have kept me occupied full-time if I'd thought it possible. My advantage was wrapped up in having a respected old farm family name and a genial way of talking to people that sometimes got them seeing other viewpoints. Being the sole heir to a fortune didn't hurt, either. Iowa folks respect hard-earned prosperity.

Anyway, once I got past brooding over the should-haves and could-haves connected with Karl's life and death, my feel-good instincts returned and I had blessings to count. The Ratchford farm did well most years, even after I began to make the changes that some people considered radical. The income, combined with my modest needs, was plentiful and well invested. It was perfect timing when Janilee stepped back into the picture.

With the future looking so rosy, my new goals were happy ones. Build a new house for my bride; let Ernest run the farm while I turned my attention to statewide endeavors; find ways to acclimate Janilee to her new/old environment and get her enthused about helping out with my conservation efforts.

BEFORE THE TWO WEEKS OF WAITING for Janilee were over, I set a late-July appointment with a group of Minnesota architects. If Janilee agreed, we could get married about then, go to Minnesota to talk with them, then go on farther north for a honeymoon in the Canadian Rockies.

"If that's what Janilee wants to do," I kept reminding myself. For too long, my decisions had been mine alone and it would take interior work to remember that my personal druthers must be modified in the future. Repeating history with a dictatorship like Dad's was no temptation.

Talking it over with Janilee during our daily phone conversations, I had found her in agreement with most ideas and genuinely receptive when I went on and on about cattle species and wind power. She did insist on something I tried to understand.

"I have built my whole adult life around the name 'Lee,'" she said. "It fits with who I am better than 'Janilee.' I don't want to come back to Iowa and have to re-invent myself. Please bear with me on this."

Okay. It made me uneasy but I could tell she wasn't casual in her demand. When I mentioned her to the Weists or someone in town, I began using 'Lee.' To my surprise, most people didn't have the problem with it that I did. After all, we had Daves and Vics and Herbs and Sals—not exactly what their mothers had in mind when they had discussed potential baby names with their girlfriends and female relatives. Saying "Lee" instead of "Janilee" was hardly worth mentioning.

Early one evening I decided to run over to the Allans. They'd been on the next farm all my life and, while I never felt particularly warm toward them, they would continue to be our closest neighbors. Besides, Caroline knew a lot of town folks from her years of teaching and would be an ideal acquaintance to help Janilee—whoops - Lee feel at home.

Timing my drop-by visit for about 7:30, I debated if it was too late. If I went over earlier, the Allans might be having supper and would feel obligated to invite me to sit down and eat with them. If I went later, they might be getting ready for bed because farm families often turn in early. This kind of delicate maneuvering so as not to put people out was part of my Midwestern heritage. I could never manage to get around it, even in circumstances when I knew that it would be better to do so.

Nowadays, I know, a lot of people go around asking for money for their pet charities and favors for their kids and advantages for themselves. Mother and Dad might have been the last generation that taught their kids to mostly not even take when it was offered—at least not without a sort of ritual dance and certainly only if they knew they could give back in the future.

Great Uncle George offers little Henry a dime for a bottle of pop.

Little Henry wants that bottle of pop with all his heart but he says to Uncle George, "Thanks, but keep it!"

This goes on two or three times before little Henry accepts the dime and scampers off to the gas station for his bottle of strawberry pop. Both parties are satisfied at the outcome. Both knew how it was going to end. If Little Henry had grabbed the dime from Uncle

George the first time it was offered, there's a chance Uncle George would be so offended at the kid's avarice that he'd never come up with another dime. If Uncle George had put the dime back in his pocket the first time Little Henry told him to, he would go down in Little Henry's memory as an old tightwad.

Still, the ritual is powerful enough to cause Little Henry to go through life very happy to give but shy about taking when he has no prospect of returning the favor.

And, therefore, here I am at the back door of the Allan's neat brick ranch house at exactly the time of evening when they don't have to offer me anything I'd be shy about accepting.

Caroline answered the door right away and asked me in. As always, the house looked as if she had just boiled it. Mother once confided to me that she found Caroline's housekeeping "sterile," but of course Caroline didn't have three men like Dad and Karl and me messing up her kitchen floor and dumping pocket debris in handy places.

Harold Allan, Caroline's husband, looked sort of like he'd been boiled, too, but that was another unkind thought for me to have. He had previously run a cattle operation even bigger than ours, but now he leased out most of his farming operation and confined his outdoor efforts to a bigger vegetable garden than two people needed. Otherwise, he didn't seem to do or say much, as far as I knew, except listen to Paul Harvey and the commodity market reports on the radio and watch the weather channel on television.

That's what he was doing this evening, slumped back in his recliner. It appeared to be raining heavily in the Texas panhandle, information he was registering with a cold, impassive expression. He nodded at me, but left the conversation to Caroline without even the obligatory grunts. He'd been down on me ever since I'd stopped planting hybrid seed corn and taken up with corn that generated its own seed.

Caroline was quick to jump into the gap.

"Ben!" she said, "I've been meaning to stop by to see you. I hear Janilee went back home."

Where she'd heard it was not a thing I would ask, but I wanted her to get things straight. "Only temporarily," I said. "Just long enough for her to resign from her job and put her house on the market. Lee is coming back pretty soon and we're planning to get married. We expect to build a new house and be moved in by this time next year."

Caroline was quick on the draw. "Oh! Janilee and I had a nice conversation last week about how handsome your house could be with some artistic remodeling! But, either way, I want to offer any expertise I have that will help you!"

I backed off, the best I could. While Caroline probably knew everything there was to know about how to make a nice home, she was a person who easily took over when she had a chance. Mother had warned me of that, years ago.

"Well," I said, "it's going to take a while to figure everything out. In the meantime, we have to spend a few months in the old house. One more Iowa winter is about all it's good for!"

Caroline got very serious and sweet-sounding then. "Ben," she said, "it is going to be so hard on her, coming from the Carolinas, to be comfortable with our weather extremes and small town ways. I want to do something for you and her, and to honor the many years we've been neighbors to your family. I'd like to give your house a really good cleaning before Janilee comes back. Then she won't have to come into a strange place with a lot of work to do. She never had the opportunity to know your family and it could be hard to make decisions about what to get rid of and what to give away!"

If I knew anything about Lee, it was that she would regard Caroline's help as an intrusion. For my part, the offer was nice enough but it involved more "taking" than I could be comfortable with. Following along with that reaction, I decided against asking Caroline to help Lee get acquainted in Ratchford. Things would just have to work themselves out.

"Thanks, Caroline. It's good of you to make such a generous offer, but we just couldn't ask such a big favor." I said, getting up to go. I addressed a comment about our own central Iowa weather in Harold's direction and headed for the door.

"Just thought I'd share the good news!" I said to Caroline.

She looked a little disappointed at my refusal and quick departure, but she grabbed a cherry pie out of her freezer and there was no way I could turn that down, too.

"Good night!" she said. "Let me know if you change your mind. Just remember, your mother would probably like to have an old friend going over her things rather than imposing on a new daughter-in-law."

"Caroline speaks Iowa real well," I said to myself, as I settled the pie into my pickup.

THE REST OF THE TIME before Lee's return went by quickly. Short days spent planning with Ernest, hiring farm help, fixing some things around the house that I'd been neglecting. Long nights spent getting paper work in order, going half-crazy with longing for Janilee.

Driving to the Des Moines airport to pick her up, I wished my truck was a shiny limousine. I wished I had hired a brass band to serenade her when she stepped off the plane. I wished I had a big hat with a long plume that I could doff when she walked toward me.

Book Four: Caroline

Dene Hellman

Thirty-Two

MINCING WORDS is not something I do well. All of my life, I have tried to understand why people don't say what they mean—or else keep their opinions to themselves.

Humor annoys me; life is no laughing matter. Other concepts that elude me are love and religion. For all the endless babble about them, neither appears to do anything helpful toward solving humanity's basic needs.

Certainly, I must concede to biological necessities but my conviction is that only the niceties of civilization, as developed through time by superior persons, make a difference in the animal kingdom. If we do not eat and dress well and observe reasonable social rituals, people are no better than a cluster of barn cats.

As soon as I saw the Jasper girls at the Ratchford school reunion, I knew they belonged in the barn cat category. I was walking over to the gymnasium entrance when their absurd car drove up.

"A convertible in Iowa is ridiculous," I said to myself. "Which one of our graduates would be so stupid?"

I didn't recognize the two women who stepped out of it, but I made several observations: these women were no spring chickens but they were acting as if they were. The younger of the pair had hair unsuitably far below shoulder-length. The older one at least had her tresses gathered up, but she was dressed like a teenager, in casual pants and a top that was designed to attract lewd attention.

Additionally, I was filled with consternation when I saw signs attached to the car that indicated some sort of psychic business.

"Fortunetellers!" I said to myself. "Probably that's the way gypsies look nowadays."

Truly, I decided these two women had been hired to be part of the evening's entertainment. If so, the alumni committee would get a piece of my mind. Slowing my pace, I let the gypsies walk into the building well ahead of me.

At the registration table a moment later, I peeled the backing off my name tag very slowly and deliberately, giving me time to ask the ladies at the reception table who the strangers were. "Why, that's Janilee Jasper, who graduated quite a few years ago! She brought her little sister Maggie along with her," they happily reported.

When I heard it was the Jasper girls, I was first shocked, then angry. Neither of them had bothered to come back to Ratchford in decades. If it had been the next year, I might have understood their attendance because that would be the centennial celebration of the Ratchford School and there would be extra folderol. But this was the nondescript 99th year and the alumni officers hadn't gone to any special trouble. The younger, Maggie, had an excuse; she hadn't graduated from here. Janilee was another matter. She had gone to school in this town right through high school. What was she now trying to prove? She had nothing but contempt for us once and that absolutely could not have changed.

However, I am a lady and, choking back my disapproval, made it a point to speak to Janilee before dinner. She was still putting on airs, after all these years. When she told me that she had eventually learned to sew, I concluded that she was either a downright liar or had no shame. If she thought for one minute that I'd forgotten the jumper incident in her freshman year, she was mistaken. I would have flunked her outright, for the semester, if Superintendent Door had not talked me out of it.

"Janilee is college material," he said. "She's going to need financial assistance and a failing mark on her record could jeopardize her scholarship eligibility. Let's have some compassion."

His mealy-mouth attitude didn't matter much to me. He'd been Ratchford's superintendent for several years and most of the town fawned on him as if he was a minor deity. In my opinion, he talked too good a game to be trusted. I couldn't figure out what personal advantage he got out of pretending affection for all the students and spending ridiculous amounts of time with parents. Nevertheless, there had to be something in it for him. Thank goodness, he hit retirement age well before I did and then went off to Texas to live closer to his son. He came back every few years to visit but hadn't in a long time. He probably had passed away; he was old enough.

In Janilee's case, I had to pretend to understand his "compassion" rubbish. What choice did I have? By this time I had been a home economics teacher in the Ratchford School for several years, and was very well thought of by the School Board and the town. If it got out that I was overly harsh, it would be difficult to live down.

NOW I TOOK CARE to seat myself over at the '50s table, so I could see what the '70s and '80s people were up to. The whole alumni gathering saw Ben Deckard walk in and behave as if he was wetting his pants when he saw Janilee Jasper. Some regarded it as the best show of the evening, if not the last 25 years. Ben was well respected in Ratchford, so what he does is always of interest and speculation. He, himself, never seems aware of the extent to which this is true. He has never shown an interest in the local girls, so some were surprised that he took up immediately with the Jasper woman and some said she had become an out-of-towner, so no surprise. I reserved judgment.

After the dinner and a rather sentimental and pointless program, I drove out to my beautiful farm home and arrived just in time to see Ben Deckard go past, his truck followed by that open psych-mobile with those two Jasper women.

"Once they get a look at that old house, ready to fall in on itself, they'll go back to where they came from," I thought.

Only those of us who have been around for years have a good idea of the Deckard wealth, because the Deckards have never been people to put on a display. Ben's father, the old skinflint, still had his original nickel held tight in his fist on the day he died. He'd trained Ben's mother to compare prices when all she wanted was a five pound bag of flour, just so his fortune wouldn't leak out anyplace. Ben, the only Deckard left this side of the graveyard, is known to be generous but we know he makes money a lot faster than he spends it.

If Janilee Jasper was anything like her mother, catching Ben would be a dream come true. She was a product of her mother's upbringing when I knew her. Hemmed in by whatever small salary Janilee's father earned clerking in the Ratchford Drugstore, the mother made up for it by training her oldest daughter like a circus seal, to show off in public. The kid had no choice but to get the best grades, be a clothes horse, and get her name in the paper for reciting all kinds of drivel at public events. If Mama could now crown her efforts by seeing Janilee catch a Deckard boy, however late in the game, she'd get off her tricycle and come back to Ratchford from that Florida sun city quicker than her daughter could count to ten.

IF THE GIRL HAD MY BACKGROUND, I thought, she would know what it is to earn her place in the world. Down in Missouri, when I grew up, there was the kind of poverty that could knock you flat for a lifetime. Unless, like me, you were super-strong inside and out and prepared to win over all odds.

Thirty-Three

My family, if you can call such a miserable bunch of losers a family, were worse than dirt-poor; they were dirt personified. We lived on the outskirts of a tiny town in the middle of the state, in the kind of squalor they write books about: tumble-down shack, weedy yard with old car bodies decorating the front of the house, a muddy pig pen in back that usually held one or two hogs for fall slaughter, and a bunch of chickens running around loose.

The house supposedly had two bedrooms but it didn't do me any good. In the winter, the heating stove kept only one or two rooms warm. I slept on a cot off the kitchen because the folks used one bedroom and my old man's two drunken brothers, Jerry and Bama, slept in the other.

The old man didn't drink so much but something ate up what little money he got from the county for digging sewer lines. Maybe it all went into Ma's belly. She was as grossly obese as anybody I've ever seen, and just sat around stuffing herself with Wonder Bread sandwiches and hog cracklings. If she ever got up off that old plush davenport, it was to go lie down on the stained featherbed in winter, or to sit on one of the broken- down chairs on the front stoop in warm weather. The only good thing the woman ever did was when she gave birth to my little brother, Billy.

Billy was so sweet. It was up to me to take care of him, which I gladly did. After school was out, I'd heat water on the cook stove for his bath and pop him into the galvanized wash tub that we used for everything from soaking Pa's overalls to cooking down lard. Afterward, I'd dry him off and read to him about the little engine that could and from other books I found at school and brought home.

But Billy got whooping cough and died when he was about five years old. The county paid to bury him and life went on, except that I hated Ma after that. If she'd taken better care of him, I reasoned, he probably would have pulled through.

Fortunately, there weren't any other kids.

By the time I was ten or eleven, maybe earlier and I didn't notice, one of my uncles had taken an interest in me. Bama was a no-good piece of work who toiled at odd jobs from time to time, then drank up his wages. He was missing a bunch of teeth and his breath stank like a pig's hind end. I should know, because he was all over me when the others weren't around. The first time I noticed it was when I woke up one night to feel his hands and mouth in places that struck me as peculiar.

After Bama realized I was awake during some of his playtime, he started going after me out in the corn crib, when I went after cobs for the stove, or in the chicken coop when I was gathering eggs.

I can truthfully say that it didn't bother me much. I was too strong to be easily hurt and, generally speaking, he could poke himself into me front or back, standing up or lying down, and it didn't matter. I had more important things on my mind and when I had enough, I batted him off.

Starting high school was one of the important things. Shabbily dressed, not too clean if the truth be known, I didn't expect to have any so-called friends. Besides, I was tall and raw-boned at a time when that look wasn't favored. My hair was mousy brown, my facial features were big and irregular, and I was so clumsy that I nearly fell over my own feet when I had to walk up to the front of a classroom.

But I got decent grades in almost everything. Whatever I have achieved is the result of being clever and having the strength of character to make the most of it. My favorite class was home economics. Mrs. Briggs, my teacher, took me in hand and made a special effort to talk to me about sewing.

"Caroline," she would say, "knowing how to sew can allow you to have the clothes you want. Fabric is not hard to come by, if you're vigilant."

Mrs. Briggs put me on to the printed cloth sacks that chicken feed came in and showed me how you could even take apart clothes other people had thrown out and salvage enough cloth to cut out a skirt or jacket. I was good at it, treadling away on the old sewing machines in the home ec room until long after school let out in the afternoon.

The problem was shoes and underwear and I solved that little dilemma by making use of Uncle Bama.

"I'm not going to let you do this anymore," I told him one Saturday afternoon when he was groping at my clothes, "unless you give me some money for stuff I need."

Bama came through, shoving a $5 bill in my hand every week or two afterward. I found it paid to show a little interest in his slobbering attentions and even suggest a variation once in a while.

The poor dope began to act like he was in love with me and that meant extra money once in a while. I got some decent underthings and shoes, then hid the rest of the money away in a hole behind the ice box.

For the first two years of high school, I took all the home economics classes that were offered. When I hit my junior year, Mrs. Briggs recommended me to some of the town ladies and I got weekend jobs helping them get ready for their bridge parties and their daughters' wedding receptions. That meant more money to save.

At home, I started cleaning things up as best I could, and even tried to rearrange the pathetic furniture and set the table nicely for supper. There still wasn't much to do with, but Pa had found a job in a shingle factory that helped pay for coal and blocks of ice for the icebox. Sometimes, I'd just catch a chicken and chop its head off, then fry it up—or stew it if it was old and tough.

Other times, when we were out of cash, we were back to a plate of sorghum to be sopped up with bread. It was hard to figure how to fix up a correct place setting for that one.

The spring of my high school graduation, I came home from school early one afternoon. As usual, Ma was settled on the davenport, her grotesque body spread out all around her.

"Caroline, Baby," she said, "go make me a peanut butter sandwich."

I did so, spreading the peanut butter disgustingly thick between two gluey slices of Wonder Bread. I cut the sandwich diagonally and put it nicely on a small plate before carrying it in to Ma.

Of course, Ma immediately stuffed practically an entire half-sandwich into her mouth and the stuff probably stuck to the roof of her mouth. She couldn't handle it and started choking. Her face turned bright red and the plate slid off her lap.

I sat down across the room watching as Ma tried to get to her feet, fell back, struggled some more while giving me beseeching looks, and then eventually quit breathing. It was her own greed that killed her, I thought. I told pa, who came in a little later, that it must have happened while I was outdoors feeding the chickens. Nobody faulted me.

The county stepped in again and Ma was buried beside Billy, in the pauper section of the local cemetery. A month later, I graduated from high school with honors. The following day I fished my money stash out of its hidey-hole, packed all my decent clothes into a couple of grocery sacks, went into town, and caught the Greyhound bus when it stopped in front of the Shell station.

Thirty-Four

Over the last year, I had worked out my plan. It was daring and, if I do say so myself, brilliant. I went over the border into Iowa.

In my early adult years, when people inquired about my family, I put on a sad face and let on that I had been orphaned as a young child. Not surprisingly, considering what no-goods they were, nobody from home ever came looking for me. Not caring to travel, I never returned to Missouri, either.

First, I got a job cooking at a truck stop outside of Council Bluffs, near the place where I'd climbed off the bus. It paid just enough to cover the cost of a shared sleeping room and I filched food from plates on their way out to the counter from the restaurant kitchen. A few truckers may have felt shorted but the waitresses heard the complaints; I didn't.

In the meantime, I sent an application to a low-cost Iowa college that had a teaching program in home economics. In my first and last risky move, I put the college admission office in touch with my high school and with Mrs. Briggs. Impressed by my grades and her glowing letter, the college offered me a tuition scholarship that left a little over $100 to pay out of pocket for the year. Naturally, funding room and board and paying for books would be my own responsibility.

A couple of weeks before the fall term was scheduled to start, I took a bus farther north to the college town and made a systematic effort to find work.

As luck would have it, the owners of a local dry goods store were willing to furnish me with room and board in return for what amounted to slave labor. I was to keep house for them, get dinner for them each night, clerk in their store in the evenings and on weekends, and teach a couple of elementary sewing classes in the store. In return, I got meals and a room to myself, the latter a luxury I'd never experienced.

Although I needed a few dollars for personal requirements and for tuition, summer jobs combined with frugal living were sufficient to get by. If it hadn't been, I'm confident that my resourcefulness would have kicked in and I'd have managed. Is it any wonder that I have always voted Republican? Simply put, where there's a will, there's a way. Those who aren't up to that are not worth the space they occupy. Republicans understand this.

There was one winter term when I just didn't have the $33 needed for my share of the tuition, and couldn't register on time. The Dean of Women called me into her office and demanded an explanation as to why I was jeopardizing my scholarship. I explained that I hadn't been paid for some work I'd done the previous summer and was short, but that I'd come up with the money in a week or two, for certain.

"College is for those who can afford it," she sneered. "You can't expect to stay on unless you pay within the week."

That was a hard time, but I had the initiative to go over to the office of the college president and asked for an appointment with him. They let me in and I explained my problem to him as two secretaries sat by transcribing the conversation on steno pads. I told him what the Dean had said. He was a nice man and he was shocked.

"Did she really say that?" he asked. I nodded "yes" and, not faking it at all, wiped away tears that were crawling down my face.

"Try to pay in the next couple of weeks," he said, in a kindly voice. I managed to do that, thanks to several customers in the dry goods store who made big purchases, big enough so I could skim off some of the dollars from the cash register that I most certainly deserved.

Quite a few years later, I happened to find myself on the campus of my old college, attending a seminar. The Dean of Women, after many years in that position, had died and a new women's dormitory had been erected, one with her name on it. "They must have been hard up for somebody to honor," I thought, wishing I could come back at night and burn the place to the ground. It required a great deal of self-discipline to walk past it each day that week, with other seminar participants, hiding my loathing for the building and the miserable name, "Matilda B. Scott," that was carved in stone above the entrance.

Actually, I enjoyed my room and board job almost as well as my college classes. The Burkes—that was the name of my employers— had a nice two-story home. Keeping it clean was no problem and cooking for them gave me a chance to try out new recipes and skills that I learned in the college home economics laboratories. They never said much, taking all that for granted, but I hadn't grown up to assess my value based on what other people said to me. What I did was for my own information and well-being and it paid off.

The dry goods store was also a pleasure. Bolts of fabric were piled half-way to the ceiling. There were rich woolens and soft rayons in addition to the colorful percales that I was more familiar with. Taking a bolt down from a shelf at someone's request, then flipping it over and over as I measured out lengths was, perhaps, the kind of satisfaction some people claim to get from sex.

I worked for the Burkes clear up until time to graduate with my B.A. and teaching certificate—with a major in home economics, if you please. They probably never found anyone as good as me to work for them after I left. I wouldn't know. After all, they had exploited me and were not Christmas card-worthy.

Thirty-Five

THE SUNDAY *DES MOINES REGISTER* always ran want ads from schools looking for teachers. All across Iowa, graduating teachers and veteran teachers, as well, perused the papers, especially in the spring and summer, to see what was available that might improve their hand-to-mouth lives. A couple hundred more dollars a year in salary or a few miles closer to their home towns were often enough to tip the balance with regard to staying where they were or going to another community. It could be said that teachers were very close to being migratory workers.

I knew what I was looking for and it was stability. Once I settled into a location I liked, it would be for keeps. My first teaching contracts took me into two different places, neither of which offered the potential lifestyle I wanted. The third school was Ratchford and it did.

Along the way, I had developed some poise, as well as a nice wardrobe of professional clothes that I tailored myself. Thanks to hair coloring, my mousy hair took on red-gold highlights. Adding a few pounds to my scrawny frame was helpful, as was increased skill with makeup. Ratchford accepted me without reservation, especially after a well-off farmer, Harold Allan, married me.

This was in keeping with time-honored tradition. New teachers were usually young women fresh from college. Either they were absorbed into the farm community as wives or they kept moving on to other towns until they got a man or resigned themselves to spinsterhood. The prettiest teacher who ever came to Ratchford married the local veterinarian, a situation I equated with sacrificing a virgin to the gods.

Harold was considered a catch, but the competition wasn't steep. He was a dry, uncreative man whose short neck stuck out at an angle from his body, a disability of unknown origin. He had passed his 35th birthday and only recently determined that a wife would be a considerable convenience. He took me to two movies in Marshalltown, accompanied me to a teachers' Christmas party, and invited me to his sister's house in Pella for dinner on New Year's Day, then asked me to marry him.

He bought me a good-sized diamond ring for Valentine's Day

when I insisted that he do so and showed him the one I wanted. He also built me a new ranch-style house on his farm when I threatened to break off our engagement if he didn't.

Harold is not stingy, just unimaginative. Every anniversary, Christmas and birthday of our married life, he has left a wad of money beside my plate when he exits the table to go do farm chores. In the early years, he said, "Go get yourself something." The words mostly ceased in time, but I could not have cared less as long as the money gifts continued in significant amounts.

At the time of our marriage, I made a vow to myself that no matter how inconvenient, I would always cook Harold's dinner and share a bedroom with him. I believed that failing on either count would be courting disaster. Thank goodness, Harold was not at all demanding in either respect.

Sex is a messy business and my inclination was to launder the sheets immediately after every episode. I was pleased when, after a few short years, it stopped. As to meals, Harold ate nearly everything, expecting only that meals occur punctually. He liked pie, very much, and it was in keeping with my professional occupation and reputation to have it available, so no difficulty there.

I never got pregnant, which suited both of us, I think; we never discussed it so, if Harold was disappointed, he never said so.

Our conversations were meager, more and more so as years passed, but we had not made a bad bargain, overall. My biggest complaint about Harold was his refusal to remove his shoes when he came into the house, forcing me into extra hours of housework. Probably, his biggest dissatisfaction with me was that I continued to teach home economics in Ratchford, year after year, saving my salary and piling up certificates of deposit in my name only.

All in all, I didn't mind having him around because structure is a very valuable asset in one's life and security can never be under-estimated. Hearing other women either complain about their spouses or laugh about their peculiarities, I made it a point to abstain from that foolishness. Instead, I frequently fabricated stories about delightful things Harold and I purportedly discussed, planned or did. It suited my chosen image of superior womanhood. Consequently, if a contest had ever been held in Ratchford to select the town's most successful marriages, very likely Harold and I would have been high on the roster of achievers.

Dene Hellman

AS THE YEARS PASSED, I began to top many a list of achievements on my own. As a teacher, my credentials were impeccable. Although I never won, several times I was nominated as State Teacher of the Year. Sadly, Ratchford was too small to have any political strength when the final choices were made, and I'm sure that was all that stood between me and that ultimate professional accolade.

Eventually, every woman in town who had been locally educated owed her skill with a sewing machine, an oven, and her home surroundings to my instruction. When night classes became popular, Ratchford's female population learned to decorate cakes, make slip covers, and arrange flowers under my supervision. I have a file drawer packed full of thank-you notes—the kind I spent years teaching them to write—testifying to my tremendous influence. Several nice scrapbooks chronicling my superiority are tastefully distributed around my house where they are sure to catch the eye of a visitor.

The oldest and most prestigious shelter magazine in the United States has, for decades, been published in Des Moines, within 30 miles of Ratchford. When I took up ornamental gardening, it wasn't difficult to arrange a spread or two about my own flower beds. Having no use for the untidiness of so-called cottage gardens, I had become skilled at developing pristine borders that held an in-season array of blooms that could be kept under control. Heaven knows, there is enough confusion in the world without promoting it in places that are supposed to add beauty.

The first time I persuaded an assistant editor from the magazine to come out to the farm to see my well-groomed landscaping, she ventured a suggestion that some readers might find it a bit too formal and cold. Assuring her that this was not so, when she came back with her boss and a photographer to make a final decision, they discovered her fears were unfounded. I had simply borrowed a well-behaved golden retriever and a pretty little granddaughter from another Ratchford teacher and they romped in the background. Fortunately, I got both of the creatures back to my associate before they did any real damage.

In the end, everyone won. My gardens photographed beautifully and the magazine could carry a low-budget story about a noteworthy garden accomplishment in their own vicinity. My colleague had the pleasure of seeing her grandchild and dog on the cover of a famous

134

publication. And my reputation as a gardener was enhanced to nearly legendary status in the surrounding area. Adding photography skills to my accomplishments, I soon began contributing little articles and pictures to small Midwestern garden magazines and they have been very well received.

AFTER ALL, MY CONSTITUENCY IS WOMEN, women as the standard bearers for civilization in rural communities. Men might be dedicated tillers of the soil, but without the enriching attention to the finer aspects of life that their womenfolk provide, rural life would never go beyond the requirements of planting, harvesting and shoveling manure.

Some people might wonder why they have been put on earth, but I have never doubted my own existence. It is to serve as an inspiration and role model for rural women.

Thirty-Six

THE DECKARDS HAVE LIVED ON THE NEXT FARM as long as I've been here, since they were married just a few years before Harold and I were wed. Karl Deckard Sr. had inherited the farm from his father, who owned several. As his only heir, his son sold off the other spreads, sticking the money in area banks, then turned around and began accumulating land adjacent to his farm whenever it was available. Once in a while he was in competition with Harold but he wasn't afraid to take chances and Harold was very cautious so Deckard usually came out ahead. Within a few years, the two of them stopped speaking to one another.

Of course, Karl Deckard could do no wrong as far as the community hotshots were concerned. They'd run out to consult him every time they had an idea. He'd tell them what he approved of and what he didn't, not even bothering to attend any meetings. And that's the way everything would end up. They totally kowtowed to his preferences, no sweat on his part.

The only time in his life he even bothered to talk to me was when the Ratchford Women's Club decided the town should have some kind of theme to put it on the State of Iowa map. With no local bodies of water except the creek that runs through the Deckard farm and joins the Skunk River father down, a landscape that is as flat as a pancake and—unlike Pella—no noteworthy ethnic group to be celebrated for its contributions, the Women's Club settled on promoting roses. Ratchford would grow them, publicize them, and hold parades and homecoming festivals with roses as a rationale.

I was certainly willing to put energy into helping organize such a venue and was, naturally, unanimously elected chairperson. It was our scheme that Deckard Sr. would provide startup money and he was subsequently approached after church one Sunday by a delegation of long-time citizens.

He listened to us without saying anything except that he'd think it over. That evening he came over to my farm. He didn't drive, just stomped down the road as if he owned it, too. I asked him in, offered him a piece of rhubarb pie—which he turned down—and sat across from him at the kitchen table.

He wasn't rude to me. In fact, he had a nasty smile plastered on his face that reminded me of Uncle Bama hefting a full fruit jar of corn whiskey to his lips.

"Let me understand this," he said. "You want to make Ratchford famous by planting roses all over town. You are aware that these expensive plants will have to be planted, fertilized and kept in good condition for months every year? You have discussed among yourselves the likelihood that they will have to be doctored for diseases, replaced after hard winters, protected from dogs, kids and cars, and baby-sat constantly by hired help?"

"Yes, we have considered those things," I answered.

"Well," said he, "I will provide the money for this effort. However, I can afford to do only so much, so I will then have to withdraw my support of the Congregational Church and the Ratchford ballpark, at the very least."

Naturally, with that kind of blackmail the Ratchford rose endeavor quickly lost steam. Then State Center took the idea up, calling itself the Rose Capital of Iowa, and that was that.

I HAVE IMMENSELY ENJOYED those rare occasions when I could see old Karl having an uneasy time of it. For example: the lovely ranch-style house that I persuaded Harold to build for me is a shining example of what a farm dwelling can aspire to, and I have always seen to it that it is kept to the highest standards. Marjorie Deckard, Karl Sr.'s wife, fell in love with it the moment she saw it and begged her husband to follow its example when, finally, they couldn't avoid repairing or replacing their generations-old farm shack.

I could have told her to save her breath. All of Ratchford knew that old Deckard wouldn't spend his cash on a new house even to assure world peace.

Marjorie was no match for him, which we also all knew, and she ended up with an old house that was now semi-remodeled by a couple of untalented local yokels, including a truly tasteless flamingo-pink bathroom that gave her husband fits.

How I wished that he was married to me! Believe me, one way or another, I would have found a method to bring him around!

LOOKING BACK, there was a brief time right after Karl Jr. was born, when Marjorie could have asked for the moon—even a pink one—and her husband would have managed to get it for her. How he doted on his baby boy! His pride was such that he even juggled the child through church services and propped him up at his side in the local café. There was a joke around town, about the time little Karl turned two, that Baby Deckard had a seat on the Ratchford Savings Bank's board of directors and his first word was, "Opposed!" Personally, I didn't appreciate such jokes. Little Karl Deckard was the most beautiful, precious child I had seen since losing my little brother Billy. He had a vigorous, well-coordinated little body, luxurious dark curls, great character in his face, and the straightest little back with perfect posture. I could empathize with his parents' devotion to him.

I virtually begged Marjorie Deckard to allow me to baby-sit. As far as I could see, she never had a moment's time to herself because her husband would never spend money on a baby-sitter or condone leaving little Karl in the care of strangers. I would have been a perfect chance for her to get away a little.

For sure, I wouldn't have charged a cent; that's how much I thought of that little boy. In this case, it went against me. Marjorie couldn't allow herself to accept such a favor.

"Oh, Caroline," she said, every time I offered, "you have too much to do as it is, with your teaching job and volunteer work."

It was regrettable. But, while I would have given much to read to that little boy and rock him to sleep, it was beneath my dignity to make a point of it. In time, I learned to keep my distance, simply taking pleasure from the times I caught a glimpse of little Karl.

He developed into a very sensitive child. Some said he was spoiled rotten and reported seeing—and hearing—temper tantrums in public places, definitely something frowned upon in our Midwestern culture. He continued to display bouts of stubbornness throughout early childhood. When he didn't want to do what his parents wished, he was even overheard sassing them.

Thirty-Seven

IT WAS AROUND THAT TIME, I believe, when Karl Sr. took matters out of Marjorie's hands and began stern disciplinary measures to bring his son into compliance. Details of his harsh training methods have never been made public, but I was once told on good authority that the Congregational preacher spoke with him about their severity. A proud man, Karl Sr. was humiliated to have his child-rearing practices a matter for discussion. The preacher was told to mind his own business and was fired the next time the church council met.

However, the two Karls came to co-exist more easily after a time. The younger Karl became a more obedient son out of fear and in later years his tendency to say little or nothing, whether his nature or learned the hard way, also helped ease the relationship with his father.

Little Karl's brother Ben, who came along three years after Karl, gained an instantly glowing reputation locally just by being the opposite of Karl. For me, there was no comparison. Karl was gorgeous and exhibited great strength of character. Ben was a perfectly ordinary looking and acting little boy who just smiled and said, "Okay!" most of the time. In my opinion, Karl had infinitely more potential. He simply needed to be parented by a mother who was less wishy-washy and a father who was more even-tempered. I would have been a perfect match for the challenges posed by Karl's temperament.

WHEN THE DECKARDS PULLED KARL OUT OF COUNTRY SCHOOL and sent him into Ratchford for his 7th and 8th grade years, I had an opportunity to take a hand in his development. Driving him home from school each day was a splendid opportunity to mentor this young man. Although I had so far missed the chance to be part of his life, I could now assume the role of a beloved aunt. The boy needed so much help in overcoming his first years that, at first, I scarcely knew where to begin.

He was very tall for his age and I knew he was an excellent natural athlete. My task would be to discover those aspects of his personality that would enable him to grow in more civilized

139

directions. It was not to be accomplished through lecturing, I finally realized. During our rides home in his 7th grade year, I talked a great deal about good manners and how a civilized structure in living contributes so much to personal well-being.

Alas, thirteen-year-old Karl merely stared out the car window at the passing scenery; I never knew if he really heard me. By chance, I made the discovery that two things he responded to were very firm praise and undemanding affection. We often stopped off at my farm house for a snack before I took him the rest of the way home. He loved my chocolate chip cookies and one day, as he munched on a plate of them, he asked if he could watch television for a little while.

"You certainly may," I said. "You are a very responsible person and have earned that privilege." Then I gently ruffled his hair, as a loving aunt would do.

His face just shone and it became a frequent occurrence after that. Some afternoons he had to go straight home and other times I had such a full schedule that I couldn't spare time to indulge him. As a result, we both particularly enjoyed the precious days when he could have his cookies and television and I could run my fingers through his hair as I'd longed to do since he was a baby. Once or twice, toward the end of the school year, we had playful little scuffles and he would end up on my lap or I on his. We were almost becoming more like schoolmates than nephew and aunt.

That summer I took to going into Ratchford the long way around, just so I would have to pass the Deckard farm and, once in a while, get to see Karl as his summer vacation progressed. He was now old enough to be of help with daily farm needs and was usually out in the fields or in the outbuildings helping his father. I saw Marjorie from time to time and always stopped to chat with her, taking care to inquire about everyone in her family with equal interest.

She would smile ruefully as she reported on her sons' growth spurts and how she was going to have to replace their pants and shoes, even before school started up again in September. I imagined that Karl Sr. would take that information hard and would be quite stingy about purchases.

On the rare occasions when I saw young Karl, I simply waved happily at him and drove on. When he returned my greeting with a wave and half-smile of his own, it just kept me walking on air for days. Marjorie was always fussing about wanting to repay me for Karl's rides home from school and, to set her mind at ease, I told her that I really could soon use some help with autumn house and garden chores. Harold, I said, was far too busy with his cattle operation to take time to clear away leaves and do a little painting and if Karl could spare an hour or two sometimes, I would be grateful.

Really, this was a bit of a joke; I was still on the young side and as big and as strong as many men. However, that fact was over Marjorie's guileless head and she assured me Karl would be instructed to repay my kindness by helping me any way he could.

At the start of his 8th grade year, Karl was larger than most and twice as beautiful. Going on fourteen, he looked as if he should begin shaving and his voice was wavering between that of a boy and that of a grown person. He was absolutely adorable.

Karl also had developed an interest in the various hoodlums who called themselves "bands," imitating one or another for my amusement alone, since his parents did not approve of this rock music mania. He was not permitted to listen to it at home.

While I could see his parents' viewpoint, it was a wonderful opportunity for me to bond with my favorite young man. Over time, I bought all the outrageous albums I could find in surrounding towns. Karl would sprawl out on my living room floor, singing along with his new heroes at times. It was very important to me to share his pleasure and sometimes I just got right down on the carpet beside him and we'd do little sing-along duets. I bought some blue jeans and low-cut shirts to slip into when we came from school and I knew he was growing up when he started sneaking peeks at my bosom.

At Christmas time, I bought him a guitar and told him it was our little secret. Needless to say, he could hardly wait until school was out in the afternoons so we could drive back to my farm. I can't say he had the talent for music that he had for the ball field, but he just loved picking away on his guitar, pretending to be part of the music scene.

He actually got some of the techniques down pretty well, writhing away in a most lascivious manner. I always praised him highly for his ability and, in truth, he must have been a quite effective performer because I began to feel strangely stirred.

One rainy Friday afternoon when we were listening to Elvis, a day that I knew Harold was spending in Waterloo at a cattle auction, I went into my bedroom, pulled off my jeans and underpants and lay down on the bed. Spreading my legs wide, I called out, "Karl, come in here. I want to show you something!"

Thirty-Eight

THE REST OF THE SCHOOL YEAR simply flew by. It was such a happy time for both Karl and me. While we couldn't have our secret moments each and every afternoon, we found time to be together very often. I have to say, Karl was a fast learner and his rush to manhood was astonishing.

When summer vacation began, we were both regretful. Karl missed his music and sneaked down the road a few times to play his guitar, listen to his records and, of course, enjoy playtime with me. He continued to gain in stature and maturity, too, which I found most stimulating.

He started high school in the fall and continued to ride home with me in the afternoon. To my dismay, we drifted into occasional lovers' quarrels. With increased outlet for his athletic talents, Karl became less enthusiastic about his guitar, and me, and sometimes refused opportunities to spend an hour or two after school in my company. If I wasn't inclined to give up our time together and drive him home, he put on a defiant face and walked between the farms.

I think it was around January when I realized that Karl had a little crush on Dotty Jessup. They shared at least one study hall that I supervised and I caught them exchanging silly notes when they were supposed to be concentrating on their books. They were very fortunate that I didn't give them detention or turn them in to Superintendent Door.

Naturally, I took steps to nip this behavior in the bud. Dotty was a little nothing who came from a wretched home environment and people who couldn't have cared less that she was attending high school. She took a home economics class that I taught and it wasn't difficult to turn the rest of the girls against her by subtly—in a kindly way, of course—suggesting she was perhaps responsible for the various little thefts of fabric and sewing notions that were now occurring.

I wouldn't have put it past the little snip to be light-fingered if she had really wanted the spools of thread and packets of trim that came up missing, so I felt no guilt about removing the items myself and throwing them into my briefcase to take home to destroy. Within two or three weeks, everyone in class was whispering, especially after I began removing uncut fabric. Goodness knows, *I* didn't personally want the stuff but it was necessary to discredit Dotty before she made a real conquest of Karl.

One afternoon she stayed after school and tried to play on my sympathy with a sobbing denial. "Miz Allan, I never stole any of those things," she pleaded.

I just looked at her sternly. "There are some very nice girls in this class!" I said. "Surely you don't want to accuse one of *them!*"

She got my drift immediately, recognizing who *wasn't* a nice girl in my judgment. Not overly enamored of school to start with, she became sullen and dropped out well before summer recess began. It was no surprise to any of us when she was seen in town the following year with no wedding ring but a very large belly. We all knew that she was going to perpetuate the miserable cycle of welfare no-goods that she sprang from.

I DIDN'T SEE MUCH OF KARL that ensuing summer, although he began a pattern that endured for many years. When, upon occasion, his male needs were exceptionally strong, he would come down the road to see me.

Perhaps because he led something of a double life, he was now permanently lapsed into near-silence. I had cautioned him repeatedly to keep our passion for one another a secret, and there was never the slightest indication that he failed his gentlemanly obligation toward me. Also, I'm sure he knew his father's temper would erupt in rage if the man found out about his son's infatuation with me.

Instead, young Karl submerged himself in athletics and farm work. The next fall, Ben came into town school and Karl began driving the both of them into Ratchford each day. I saw no evidence that he developed any more crushes on the high school girls. Surely, he recognized that they were shallow children compared with my adult virtuosity. Once in a while, he even sought me out in my home economics laboratory, half-shoving me into hidden corners and then nearly tearing my clothes in his haste to make love. Actually, I liked it, although I always protested a little. At times, I would reciprocate, leaving bite marks in places that would have forced him to do some creative explaining if his coach or one of the other team members caught sight of them in the locker room.

Unfortunately, Karl became increasingly surly. If I protested, he would reach for the most provocative warning he could find, threatening to go to Mr. Door and tell him everything about us. It saddened me to be forced to counter his threat with one of my own.

"In the first place," I said to him, "no one would believe you or take your word against mine. If necessary, I can easily prove that you have repeatedly raped me and I have not informed on you out of respect and friendship for your parents. I am highly regarded in this community, whereas you are known to be difficult to get along with."

Thank goodness, Karl understood this reasoning and his threats stopped even as our little trysts continued to occur from time to time.

WHEN KARL GRADUATED it was now my task to get on with my life. It had been my hope for several years that at this point we would find a way to be together permanently. I had a good bit of money saved and was willing to make the sacrifice required to begin a new life. It was a hope I now set aside, at least temporarily. He was not considering college, thank goodness, and appeared content to completely sink into farm life. As far as I knew, he only went into town to play on the Ratchford baseball team. But, as long as he lived on the next farm, I retained a measure of optimism.

Not allowing myself to dwell on what some would consider a frustrating situation, I permitted myself a growing role in community life. My influence linked from high school classes to the weddings and baby showers of former pupils to night school courses where these young women and their mothers and grandmothers learned many of the finer aspects of social and cultural life under my tutelage. They were truly "my" ladies and the source of much pride for me. There was no comparison between a tea put on by one of my Ratchford protégées and that of a group from another town. My scrapbooks fattened, generously illustrated by my photography.

AN OUTBREAK OF AWARD GIVING overcame Ratchford. Some perfectly dreadful people who shared the physical biology of my ladies and me began whooping it up about the "women's movement." They were behind the rest of the country by a good number of years but Ratchford people are disinclined to adopt fads.

I had always regarded this so-called feminist cause as complete nonsense. Any woman who was worth her salt surely knew enough to go after what she wanted and move mountains until she got it and I, for one, had no respect for anyone who didn't. The endless propaganda about the rights of farm inheritance, equal pay and freedom from domestic violence was ridiculous. I knew of no one in Ratchford who suffered from inequities and spousal violence and if Harold had dared to raise a hand to me or refuse to put my name on the deed to the farm, I would have found a way to make him very sorry.

At any rate, these later-day women's movement persons decided to hold an award ceremony in Ratchford, specifically to honor someone who had done much to better life for Ratchford's women. They called for nominations from the community.

This caused me to pick up my ears. In truth, there were few long-time female residents of Ratchford who had worked within the community as diligently as I had been doing for years. If anyone deserved that award, it was me. Nevertheless, it was simply amazing that this had to be pointed out to the very people who were capable of sending in literate nominations. And it had to be done very subtly, of course.

"Who do you think should be named as recipient of the Minerva Award?" I asked the self-important wife of the local osteopath.

She thought for a moment, then said, "How about Marie Schall? She took in all those foster children and they all turned out a credit to her raising."

I cast my eyes down and said, hesitatingly, "Good idea! If she had just—but never mind—it is none of my business."

"What? What?" Mrs. Osteopath replied. "Is there something I don't know?"

"I think bygones should be bygones. After all, people change," I said.

Then Mrs. Osteopath's face lit up and she said, as if a brilliant revelation had occurred, "Caroline! Your name should certainly be placed in consideration! Why didn't I think of it before?"

I can't tell you how many of those tiresome little chats were necessary before some enterprising and well-organized soul took it upon herself to write the nomination letter on my behalf.

The upshot is that when the first Minerva Award was handed out in Ratchford, I walked across the dais of the Ratchford Holy Trinity Lutheran Church to receive it. There were many photographs and congratulatory stories in the area newspapers; the organization behind the women's movement people saw to that, even getting a report into the *Des Moines Register*.

The following year the winning Minerva Award nomination was signed and filed jointly by the wives of both community pastors, not an influence to be taken lightly. The award recipient was Ethel Baines, who had fought against pro-abortion legislation in six states and Washington, D.C. Old Ethel had even made *Time Magazine* for shoving a rubber fetus in the face of a Supreme Court Justice with liberal leanings. She was greatly admired, locally.

The women's rights persons seemed to be really discouraged after that and didn't hold any more Minerva Award ceremonies. However, I had my little plaque on my dining room wall and in later years, whenever I had to submit biographical information to some entity, I took care to mention it.

Award fever caught on though, and soon a proliferation of plaques, certificates and statuettes testified to eminence in every walk of life. I am happy to say that a wide variety of those graced my home within a few years.

Thirty-Nine

THE FOLLOWING YEARS were actually quite pleasant. Karl kept to himself but found a way to visit me from time to time—often enough for me to appreciate his tremendous virility but not so often as to be inconvenient.

It began to be rumored around Ratchford that young Karl Deckard was insane. He was seldom seen, but those who caught a glimpse of him reported that his hair had grown long, that he never spoke to anyone, and that old Karl Sr. had complained that he needed to put in extra-long work hours because his son was becoming undependable.

Ben came back to the farm to stay, without the lovely woman he had married. That was too bad. She and I had enjoyed a certain amount of rapport, an unusual situation for me. I simply thought she had her head on straight, knew what she wanted and had gone after it. Ben, however, didn't seem to miss her after they split, so perhaps he had been unworthy of her abilities. She was certainly superior to Janilee Jasper. She and Ben would have been a marvelous team and I would have enjoyed mentoring her.

Then, to make matters worse, Karl got embroiled in some Pentecostal church that had sprung up in Des Moines. His father had died, which was no cause for mourning to most Ratchford people, and Karl now stopped visiting me entirely. Sometimes, when I came home from an evening event, I would drive past my farm and down to the Deckards. I knew which upstairs room was Karl's and I'd slow my car down to a crawl so I could look into his lighted room and see him. Usually, he was at his desk, attentive to some writing project.

One Sunday morning when I knew he would pass by on his way to Des Moines, I actually went out to the road in front of our house and waited by the mailbox. When his truck came along, I stepped right out in front of it, risking life and limb. He had to stop, naturally, to keep from running me over. "How are you, Karl?" I asked. Frankly, they were the only words that came to mind.

Karl leaned his head out of the cab. "You whore of Babylon!" he rasped.

"I know you now for what you are. You tempted me when I was a child, and you have lain in wait for me all of my life, like the evil viper you are. Your reign is over. I have taken steps to expose you to the world!"

Then he put the truck in gear and drove down the road, kicking up gravel as he went.

Well! It did take me a half-hour or so to regain my composure but I made a pot of coffee and sat down at the kitchen table to think through what I had just heard and, if necessary, come up with a plan of action. The man was out of his mind and might possibly follow up with lurid accusations against me. The words "child abuse" had become popular and there were always sick-minded people ready to point fingers at their betters.

In my case, probably, the people of Ratchford would consider the source and ignore his ravings. However, they always enjoyed a good story and would report every detail of an especially juicy one to everyone they knew. My reputation would suffer to some degree. I was not far from retirement and didn't relish the prospect of becoming an object of conjecture just when I should be basking in the glory of a life well lived.

Twice in the ensuing weeks, I went over to the Deckard farm when I knew Marjorie and Ben were gone and sought Karl out. The first time, I found him in the machine shed and went right up to him, laying a hand gently on his arm. He shrugged it off and repeated the ugly words he had used in our Sunday morning confrontation. The second time, that old fool Ernest Weist, whom Ben had hired to help out, came ambling into the barn when I was looking for Karl. He hung around until I gave up and went home.

In truth, I wondered if he had overheard something the other time I was there. I am not given to paranoia, but I sensed he had developed a peculiar attitude toward me. Even in the years after Karl Jr.'s death, whenever I went to the Deckard farm Ernest would wander out of nowhere into the farmyard and make a dumb remark, usually about the weather. He never said anything out of the ordinary, but sometimes I got the idea that he had peculiar thoughts. The time I stopped to see Janilee, a few days after the high school reunion, is an example. When I drove up and parked the Buick old Ernest came skulking out of the tool shed and waved his forefinger at me in acknowledgment of my presence.

HE DIDN'T NEED TO WORRY; I wasn't after Janilee. What I did want was a refresher course in how the inside of the house was laid out. When she asked me in for coffee, I remembered. The stairs to the upstairs bedrooms were ugly and utilitarian, located off to one side between the kitchen and the hall. My inner demand for niceties caused a little shudder to run up my spine at such a miserable placement.

There was one really pleasant moment and it happened when Janilee and I were scouting the yard for the unlikely presence of interesting plants.

I hadn't been aware that the Deckards had a cistern. I knew all about those wells from growing up in Missouri. Where we lived, every rural acreage and farm had one, sometimes hand-dug down to 25 or 30 feet. They had their uses—collecting water in times of drought, especially. When they weren't in use, they were great hiding places for stuff you didn't want to see again and handy drowning places for the kittens that kept showing up in the barn, thanks to randy old toms and female cats squalling in lascivious heat.

I shoved the reinforced concrete cover off the Deckard cistern and was somewhat disappointed to find it had been filled in. Janilee's startled look when I pushed the cover off was pleasure enough, however. It didn't go amiss to let her know that I had that kind of strength. If need be, there wasn't a man this side of a hotshot Des Moines gym who would be a match for me, even a youngish Iowa farmer.

It was amusing, when I drove off for home, to see old snoopy Weist come out of the barn shadows and head up to the house to see Janilee. What was he afraid of? One day, he and I might have to reach an understanding.

BEFORE HIS DEATH, I made one more effort to reason with Karl. A chance encounter with Ben in the grocery store had yielded the information that he was going to an out-of-town seminar for a couple of days. Waiting until I saw Ernest out working in a field far from the Deckard farmhouse, I put on a jacket, hat and gloves against the nippy, windy day and ducked around behind my house, tramped through the adjoining fields, picked my way through the untidy old orchard and went around the back of the Deckard house. I wasn't sure just what I'd say to Karl when I found him but knew it had to be persuasive.

He was in the cow barn when I located him. Surprisingly, he looked totally competent and at peace. He had a young heifer in the squeeze chute and was preparing to administer medication of some sort. He had a syringe in his hand and was about to stick the needle in her. As I came in through the side door and spoke his name, he startled, tripped, and fell, still holding the syringe.

I am not a person who needs time to make decisions and act. Quick as a wink, I reached down and, grasping the syringe, thrust the needle as far as it would go into Karl's groin. He tried to stagger to his feet but every time he did I shoved him down on the barn floor. He was a big man but I am a big woman and light on my feet, so I was able to elude his hands when he tried to grasp me by the ankle.

Karl began to wheeze and gasp, looking up at me wildly and making noises as if he was either pleading or threatening. In no time at all, he lay still and stopped all the useless struggling.

Thanking my lucky stars that I was wearing gloves, I rearranged the syringe and his limbs a little, then cut out the back way once again and hiked home through the orchard and back fields.

I held my breath a bit as, sometime later, I heard the ambulance and then saw the sheriff's car careen past toward the Deckard farm. Fortunately, freak accidents are more usual than uncommon on farms, and talk dwindled within weeks after Karl was safely underground in the Ratchford cemetery. A sheriff's deputy always claimed he'd found the syringe suspiciously positioned when he went to the death scene. Because of that, a small but persistent rumor suggested that Karl had deliberately killed himself. It would not have surprised the good citizens of Ratchford if that was the case but, for Marjorie's and Ben's sake, the thought was suppressed in polite society.

MARJORIE DECKARD WENT DOWNHILL fast after that. Two deaths in her family, her husband's and her son's, one after a lingering illness and the other a shock, took away much of her purpose for living. I was regretful, to be sure, that Karl was no longer of this world but it was certainly for the best.

THERE WAS A LARGER CONCERN on my part. Karl was gone, but what had he left behind by way of incriminating remarks? What, I asked myself, had he been so industriously writing during his final months? At a decent interval after the funeral, I went over to see Marjorie. Damage control might be indicated.

There are times, these days, when hugging is necessary. It is not in my nature to partake of this latter day custom. In fact, I yearn for past years when a simple handshake was sufficient to convey general good will. Nevertheless, I yielded to the encroaching culture and took Marjorie in my arms. She cried, assuming my affection and concern was that of a nearly lifelong neighbor. I dabbed at my dry eyes when she at last relinquished her hold on me.

"Marjorie," I said, "allow me to be of help. I know you must find it hard to deal with concluding Karl's affairs. As an old friend, I'd be glad to clear out his room for you."

"Thank you, Caroline," said Marjorie. "I know you and Karl grew to be friends during the years you brought him home from school. But for the time being, it is all too much for me to face. I've just left Karl's room as is and closed the door. Sometime later, I'll face what should be done and, if I need help, I'll call you."

Very good. I think she was terrified of finding something akin to a suicide note and chose the easiest path of denial. For my part, it made me most uncomfortable to think of what diaries or journals or letters Karl might have been penning at the time of his death. Since I'd known him as a high school student, as well as a lover, I knew he was no Shakespeare and would not have been indulging any creative ambitions.

Nevertheless, he could put nouns and verbs together with the degree of competence appropriate for an Iowa farmer. If he had something to say, he could do it with some degree of clarity.

After Marjorie moved into Ratchford, all remained quiet. She may have meant to come back out to the farm when she felt better, but didn't. When she died a couple of years later, all was still serene. Seeing one more chance to get into Karl's room, I then approached Ben with the open graciousness of a long-known friend.

"Ben, you're alone on the farm now and there must be dozens of things demanding your attention," I said. "I knew your parents for many years. Please let me relieve you of one burden by cleaning up the farmhouse and dealing with your mother's clothing and personal effects. Since her sister isn't up to the job, I know it would be her preference to have a long-time woman friend do this for her and for you."

But Ben also refused my help. "I'll get to it one of these days," he said.

THERE WAS NO IMMEDIATE DANGER, I realized. Ben was

generally regarded in the area as a fine man without many faults, but I knew that compulsive tidiness was not a strength of his. In fact, he was quite uninterested in anything that didn't involve his harebrained ideas about organic farming and conservation. Marjorie had made several joking comments over the years about trying to make her son sort through the clutter of books, music, business files and correspondence that mushroomed around him. Tackling the leftover belongings of the deceased, no matter how dear to him the departed had been, would not be a lead item on his to-do list.

But, reluctant to leave it totally to chance, I went to the Deckard farm several times during the ensuing years, timing my visits for days when I'd seen Ben drive past on his way to other places.

My aim was simply to enter the house, go to Karl's old room, and remove anything of a personal nature that might compromise me. How much better for all of us if that had occurred! Unfortunately, the front and back doors were always locked. There isn't much fear of intrusion around Ratchford, but grain and livestock theft is an occasional hazard and farm people tend toward caution with regard to access. Additionally, Ernest Weist, the interfering old coot, was often at the farm and the minute I drove in, he'd be out in the farmyard telling me Ben was away. Then he'd stand there, always with that polite simpering smile on his face, until I drove off.

It occurred to me that setting fire to the Deckard farmhouse might be an ultimate necessity. I've always been partial to fire as a purifying agent and the building would certainly go up in consuming flames, like the pile of kindling it was, with very little encouragement. It probably didn't have much insurance coverage, if any, so no interfering investigators would come around.

Forty

THESE CONCERNS DID NOT totally inform my life. Retirement found me busier than ever because there was time to reach out to neighboring communities in my zest for good works. It just astounded me how much influence I could exert simply by filling in the gaps left by people with insufficient time or energy to step up and do the things that needed doing. Hospital gift shops, fund-raising luncheons, a myriad of senior craft shows—all benefited from the time I could now devote to them.

Harold held on. He was in his eighties and had leased out the farm land on shares. He liked to keep some control over the cattle operation but mostly concentrated ridiculously on a personal vegetable garden in back of the house. It was beyond me what pleasure he could possibly derive from tottering into the house clutching a tomato he seemed to regard as a triumph of gardening skills. Still, he was not much trouble and I put up with him. The time had passed for me to benefit from his demise. If he became too troublesome, however, I would have sent him off to the Ratchford Nursing Home before he knew what was happening. I had directed my life entirely too carefully to waste precious time dealing with a senile or incontinent old man.

THIS WAS THE QUIET STATE OF AFFAIRS until the last Ratchford school reunion when Janilee Jasper showed up and complicated things. She had her hooks into Ben Deckard before a day passed, and then she became a permanent threat.

I breathed easier when she went back to wherever in the South she came from. But when Ben came over to our place and said she was going to come back to Ratchford for good, as his wife, it changed everything.

From his besotted comments, I gathered that Janilee would be flying into Des Moines the following Friday. In turning down my offer to prepare the house for her, he also gave the impression that a priority for them—her, actually—would be clearing out Karl's room. That gave me little time to plan appropriate action, but plan I did.

On Friday, I took up my watch. Since it stayed light for so long in summer evenings, I was somewhat inconvenienced. My signal to act depended on seeing the light go on in Karl's room. However, my logical mind took into account the reuniting of two lovers after a period of many days. Without doubt, they would fall into one another's arms at the airport and barely make it back home before transporting themselves to bed and bliss. Saturday or Sunday were the logical times for any nest-organizing they would undertake.

SATURDAY CAME and I saw them drive by around noon, then return just before dark in the evening. I was inclined to think they had multiple errands in Des Moines or one of the smaller county seat towns, would be tired or lustful or both upon their return, and that the following day, Sunday, would be when my vigilance was required.

FORTUNATELY, SUNDAY WAS A DARK, GLOOMY DAY with rain falling in sheets every couple of hours and drizzling the rest of the time. Since I needed to turn my own kitchen light on to see across the room, it was a sure thing that if Ben and Janilee were going to begin work on Karl's room, the light I'd been watching for would go on in there.

In the early afternoon I picked up my camera and told Harold I planned to go outside and do some photography. This was more information than he wanted or needed, but I had my reasons for providing it. Then, after paying a visit to the vet room in the cow barn, I climbed into my Buick and headed down the road toward the Deckard place. When I came within sight of the farmhouse I slowed, then stopped. I began strolling along the roadside, my trusty Olympus in hand, snapping pictures of the early Queen Anne's Lace as its blossoms sparkled with raindrops. Only a few cars passed, but I always waved happily at their occupants. Area farm people knew me and had a lot of reverence for my flower photography. They would feel an extra special connection when my pictures of Queen Anne's Lace, bespeckled with raindrops, showed up in the next *Iowa Today* magazine. They would, I knew, cut out the article and send it to relatives in North Dakota. "Our neighbor," they would scrawl, drawing a circle around my name.

My patience was rewarded. In late afternoon, just as I'd predicted, the light went on in Karl's room.

I called Harold on my cell phone. Unaccustomed to calls from me, he answered with "Huh?" and I said, "I'm just wet through and through. I'm going to stop by the Deckard farm to say 'Hi' to Ben and his bride and then I'll be right home to fix supper." I was rewarded with another "Huh?" Not important. I wanted my call on record.

Hastily, I returned to the car and drove to the Deckard farm, parking unobtrusively under a big tree, as much out of sight of the road as possible. Ernest Weist's disgusting old truck was parked over by the barn, even though it was Sunday. He had come to tend to afternoon chores, no doubt. I would have to hurry.

It had stopped raining but the sky was very still, promising more to come. I crossed the front yard, went around to the back, entered through the unlocked door into the ugly kitchen, and set down a box of matches and the gasoline can I had retrieved from the Buick's trunk.

Quietly, I climbed the stairs. Janilee and Ben were in Karl's room. They had evidently removed some things from the wall because she was busy ripping apart some nasty old posters and stuffing them into a garbage bag. Ben was bent over Karl's old desk, had opened it, and was adjusting some reading spectacles on his nose, the better to examine its contents.

"Good afternoon!" I said, stretching my face into a pleasant smile. "May I help you with your task?"

Both Ben and Janilee whirled to face me. She simply looked surprised but he looked positively angry. "When did you come in, Caroline?" he asked. "What can we do for you?"

"A truly discourteous way for one neighbor to address another," I said.

Just then, a woman's voice shouted loudly from downstairs, "Lee! Lee! Are you here?"

Janilee looked astonished. "That's Maggie!" she said. Rudely pushing me aside, she ran out the bedroom door before I could stop her. I could hear her shout, "Maggie! Is that you?" as she clattered down the stairs.

With a bewildered look on his face, Ben prepared to follow her. Whatever the circumstances, I simply could not allow that to happen. Reaching into my raincoat pocket, I withdrew one of the loaded needles and syringes I'd taken from the veterinarian supplies in our cow barn and quickly stepped toward him.

155

Dene Hellman

Book Five: Maggie

Forty-One

THE STUDIO PHONE RANG ONCE, stopped, rang again, stopped, rang a third time.

"Is that one client or three?" I asked myself as I stepped over the paws-and-belly-in-the-air body of a sleeping cat.

It had, so far, been a quiet morning. The Fourth of July, with all of its flourishes, had passed but left some debris trailing behind it. I don't know what it is about holidays that causes so much uproar in peoples' heads, but any day marked for serious observance brings an avalanche of psychic consultations.

I tend to blame it on early grade school years when teachers have their classes coloring, cutting and pasting the Santas or hearts or flags appropriate to the upcoming festivity. "Special. Special. Special. Anticipate. Anticipate. Anticipate," goes the message and lots of people never get over holiday expectations.

Then, when the sun comes up in its usual place and wishes don't get fulfilled, tears of disappointment flow and anger rises. I have been yelled at on Christmas by an endless string of unhappy people who don't really want a consultation, just somebody to take their frustrations out on.

"WHY," shrieks the woman in Oregon, "didn't I get a diamond ring from my boyfriend?"

"Because," I'm sometimes tempted to say, "he doesn't like you anymore and I can understand why."

But that would be unprofessional so I shuffle the cards. "I see that you need to reassess his feelings for you," I say, in all honesty.

BANG goes the phone on the other end and I consider whether I should just shut down for the rest of the day before I alienate any more people.

But today is a normal Sunday and my business phone has been quiet until now. Maybe my clients are all in church praying for what they want. I answer on the third ring, "Sister Angelica. How can I help you?"

"Maggie?" a man's voice asks.

This startles me. I don't use "Maggie" in my professional work, except in my home territory with my local clients.

"Yes?" I answer, puzzled.

"Maggie!" the voice repeats, more firmly.

"I've heard that voice before," I think, searching through my internal catalog of voice-prints. It belongs to an older man. The pronunciation is Midwestern and a hint of formal education clings to it.

"Who is this?" I ask.

The question is ignored. "Maggie, get down to Iowa right now and get them out of that house," the man says, with no-nonsense diction.

The line goes dead and I put the phone down slowly.

"That wasn't a joke," I say, addressing the previously sleeping cat who is now awake and staring at me.

Then I get scared.

I sit down in the club chair and consider.

This call came in on my business line, the one I use for psychic consultations. It is from someone who knows me and whose voice is vaguely familiar, probably professional.

Another psychic? The message itself is perfectly clear. Go to Ben's farm in Iowa and get Lee and Ben out of the farmhouse. Do it immediately. I know that Lee is there because she and I talked only a few days ago when she was aiming to fly back North. Unless she'd been kidnapped from an airport someplace, she is definitely in Iowa.

Will I ignore this call or accept it as valid?

It is 9:30 on a Sunday morning. Jack is out fishing with his brother, there are seven animals to tend to, and I hate driving the interstate roads. I have no idea who is telling me to do this thing and I'd like an excuse to get out of it. If only I could call Lee to discuss!

"Damn Lee for not having a cell phone," I think. It is another one of our sisterly differences of opinion, with me pro-cell and her anti-cell.

"I'm hounded enough at work," she has always said. "With no family left at home, why should I hand over my private time to business associates? Unless I'm traveling for business, my phone stays at home."

It's useless for me to go looking for Ben's phone number. If I'd ever had it, I don't now. And no use calling Information because, when I try to recall Ben's last name, I come up blank.

"Hi, ho!" I say to myself. "I'm going to Iowa!"

First, I call Jack, hoping he hasn't turned off his phone or left it in the pocket of a jacket that's back in his truck. Knowing how skeptical he can be about my chosen vocation, I don't bother to give him details.

"Jack," I say. "I've heard Lee is down in Iowa and something has come up. I don't know what. Maybe she wants to get married right away. Anyway, she needs me to come down there this afternoon."

I hold the phone away from my ear to tone down the sound of Jack's sputtering.

"Uh huh." "Uh huh," "Uh huh," I say to warnings about gas and oil levels, tire pressure, and speed limits.

"I'll call you tonight," I promise. "Probably I'll be back in a day or so. Walk the dogs. Water the planters on the deck. See 'ya!"

AFTER DUMPING A COUPLE DAY'S WORTH OF CLOTHES into an overnight bag, I went out to consult with Max. He had enjoyed some time off since Lee and I got back from Iowa a few weeks ago. I had treated him to some rehab to remove the Iowa gravel dust from his exterior and innards and packed him into his unglamorous tool shed/garage for a well-earned rest.

Now, I poked around in his glove compartment for the maps Jack had carefully stowed there last month.

I hate maps. I hate unfolding them, the pretense of trying to read them, the outrage of folding them up again into the neat packages in which other people expect to find them. Thank you very much, I know "up" is north, "down" is south, and "left" is west. It's the squiggly lines in between that confuse me. One of these days I should go buy one of those guidance systems that *tell* you what to do but I rarely drive anyplace that I don't already know how to navigate. Besides, Max would probably resent having his territory invaded by a stuck-up being that pretended to know everything. *"Turn left at the next corner,"* would be an all-around annoyance and insult to both of us.

Getting to the Iowa state line was the first challenge. I knew there was no way in hell I could avoid that bridge over the Mississippi River, but it would be nice not to have to drive on four-lane interstate highways. Someone had once said there is a way down to Iowa that goes around Baraboo and Spring Green but, no matter how long I stared at the map, I couldn't figure out how to do it. There was no alternative choice for me and I had to face the fact that since I do know how to get from Boxville to Madison, I should do that and pick up the Interstate there, praying there would be no road construction or detour.

Forty-Two

AFTER BACKING MAX OUT OF HIS SHED, I sat in the driveway for five minutes, gritting my teeth while trying to fold the map, then dumped it, unfolded, onto the floor of the back seat. This wasn't a gleeful top-down excursion, so I put the top up. Waving goodbye in the general direction of the kennel, where all three dogs were lined up on their hind legs watching me and wagging their tails, I took off.

"This is a test. This is a psychic test to see if you trust your gift of insight enough to believe crazy messages from unidentified messengers," drummed in my head for the first 30 miles. Then I let it go, focusing on covering the miles. It wasn't a nice day. It was way too hot and bursts of raindrops smacked the windshield, first at intervals, then settling into a torrent. My five hour trip was for sure going to take extra time.

In Madison, I negotiated the horror that is called "merging" with a shameful lack of self-confidence, behaving as if a stop sign visible only to me was perched at the end of the entrance ramp. This drove all oncoming drivers, not to mention the ones behind me, to an orgy of gesturing.

I was no sooner on the four-laner when the rain got so heavy that it was hard to see who I was sharing the road with. Semi-trucks with superiority complexes swept past, throwing up walls of water that I tried to peer through. During one of those peering-intervals my eyes dropped to the gas gauge. It read on the "Empty" mark; I had forgotten to drop by the convenience store for a tank of gas on my way out of Boxville and now I was going to have to face serious consequences.

More terror. The rain came down, the semi truckers honked viciously as they passed me, and I crept along trying to recall how much reserve Max's tank was supposed to hold after it announced it was empty. And, for God's sake, it was the Interstate. No friendly little towns with nice little gas stations and cashiers to reassuringly call me "Honey."

There was a big plaza somewhere along here, I recalled, with many gas pumps, sundries, even a section with fast food items. Would it come up soon enough to save me from sure death under the wheels of an 18-wheeler?

And then, there it was. The plaza wasn't lit up but I saw it and actually made the proper exit turn off the highway that brought it close. "Wow! Maggie and Max, the Olympic driving team," I said, wheeling up to a gas pump.

Exactly nothing happened after I pushed in my debit card. The pump didn't pump so I went inside to see why not. "Storm outage," said a man behind the "pay here" cage. "The back-up will kick in pretty soon. Why don't you go have a cup of coffee?"

That's what I did for half an hour. With the flip-flops my stomach was doing, there was no temptation to order food, so I just hunkered down at a table sipping from a Styrofoam cup that crunched as I took frustrated nips out of its rim. It was sort of pleasurable, though, to see truck drivers, probably the same ones who had so rudely honked at me, slouched at their own tables while staring ferociously at their shipping logs. When the lights popped on sometime later, we all jumped to our feet and raced out to the pumps.

Once on the road again, with the rain letting up for the most part, the distance to the Mississippi River was covered uneventfully. At the bridge, I gulped. When Lee had made me drive over it in June, I'd been tempted to shut my eyes and hope for the best. Now, I was grateful for the experience. Carefully, I picked my way across.

Once through Dubuque, it was map time again but I avoided that by going into smaller gas stations that might be staffed by friendly people. No fool I, I never asked for directions to the middle of Iowa. Instead—remembering the towns we'd passed through in June—I just asked for the directions to the next one down the road. In that fashion, I drawled across Iowa, a frog leaping from one lily pad to another for what seemed like hours until—oh how magnificent are the ways of the Universe—a sign saying "Ratchford" loomed up at the side of a decent blacktop road.

I made it to a Citgo station on the edge of town, knowing somebody was going to have to tell me how to get to the Deckard farm. "You're lucky you stopped here," said the laid-back guy who was running the place. "You just take this gravel road running north past the station and head out of town for five or six miles until you get to County D. Make a left turn, go down two or three miles. It will be the third farmhouse on the right. Name is on the mailbox."

Now those were my kind of directions! Max didn't need feeding at the moment so I bought a can of ginger ale and a pack of gum by way of thanks. As I headed out the door, the nice fellow said, in sort of a concerned-but-minding-his-own-business voice, "We've had some pretty crazy weather today. Lots of rain and then some hail a couple of hours ago. Take your time and be on the lookout for anything unusual."

"I can't be more than half an hour away from Lee," I thought. It was close to 4:30 and the sky looked unfriendly but quiet. I was hungry but not about to waste time by hunting up a restaurant or a McDonalds or whatever Ratchford might have to offer its population.

"Hope whatever is so urgent doesn't mean we can't have supper at a decent time," I said to Max. Like the gentleman he is, he purred back into action and took off north of town as we had been instructed.

Even at gravel-road speeds, we were at the County D turnoff in no time. For a summer afternoon, it was getting dark in a nasty way. The ditches along D were filled with water, so I knew the recent downpour had been colossal. I passed the first farm, then the place with "Allan" on the mailbox.

"I wonder how the old high and mighty retired teacher is going to like having Lee as a neighbor," I remarked to Max.

We came up on the one-lane bridge that spanned the little creek that runs through Ben's farm, and County D took on a squishy feel. I slowed Max down to a crawl because, today, the little creek wasn't little anymore. Water was running beneath the bridge in a torrent that threatened to rise up and cover the road.

Patting Max as if he was one of my dogs, I crept out onto the floor of the bridge. Horrified, I heard it talk back in ugly creaking noises. My powers of insight kicked in.

"This bridge is going to buckle," I thought, "and I can't get to the farm if it does."

Relying on pure instinct, whether psychic or no, I backed Max up to more solid road, then gunned him with my gas-pedal foot to the floor.

Max flew across and we landed on the other side just as the whole bridge structure collapsed into the racing water of the creek.

"No time to think about it," screamed my brain as I tore down the mile or so to the Deckard farm.

The house was there but there were no lights to be seen through that god-awful picture window. I pulled into the farmyard where Ben's pickup and a big fancy Buick stood side by side.

The air was very still as I got out of Max and raced to the back door; the sky was turning a brutal blackish-yellow. Yanking the door open, I hollered "Lee! Lee!" as loudly as my lungs could manage.

Forty-Three

LEE CAME RUNNING down the stairs and across the kitchen. "Maggie! Is that you?" she shouted. Every few steps she looked back over her shoulder and called, "Ben?" I grabbed her hand and pulled her out the door, kicking back the screen door with the heel of my foot.

The sound of a freight train barreling down the tracks penetrated the air; I knew what it was. I had lived in the Midwest all my life and hardly a year had passed without hearing about some town or trailer park being wiped out by a tornado. There was one coming in our direction right now and Lee and I had to get to someplace safe, and quickly.

An old man came running across the yard from one of the farm buildings. Grabbing Lee and me, he half-dragged us across the yard to a ditch depression that fronted the road. Disregarding the fact that it held several inches of water, he threw us down into it, our heads propped on the bank, then threw his body across ours. We could see over the edge but there was no chance he would let us up out of there, no matter what.

What followed was beyond immediate comprehension. A funnel cloud dipped. The house tore apart and crumpled, then only seconds later there was a second explosion and flames shot up in all directions from the wreckage.

Lee started screaming, "BEN! BEN! BEN!" and began pounding on the old guy who was holding us down. He let go of me but doubled his hold on her, which was fortunate because she would have gone tearing off into the fire if he hadn't.

The tornado had danced away from us and was on its way somewhere else as we dragged ourselves out of the ditch, Lee still screaming like a madwoman as the man and I stared, speechless, at the flames. They consumed most of the house immediately and were already dying down as debris fell into the basement.

Trusting that Lee was being restrained by our rescuer, I recovered my balance enough to look around. That tornado had been mighty selective. The farm buildings looked to be intact. Max and the Buick hadn't been touched, nor had Ben's truck, but the old farm swing was perched on top of a big tree that stood between the road and the farmyard. Looking across the ruins of the farmhouse, I could see that the orchard of old trees that had stood behind it had been knocked flat.

Lee kept on screaming hysterically and I reached across the old guy and slapped her hard across the face. "Shut up!" I said. Then I walked over to Max, retrieved my cell phone and pushed the emergency button.

"Deckard farm," I said into it. "House blew down, then burned up with somebody in it. You can't come down County D. The bridge is out."

The old guy was still hanging onto Lee, a grip he didn't loosen at any time. She had taken to vocalizing kind of a cross between sobbing and howling. I'd never heard anything like it and the sheer horror of the sound made me think of all the old stories about Hell.

The guy, too, had a look on his face that said this was beyond any garden-variety nightmare. Thank God, the fire trucks and rescue vehicles arrived as soon as they did, before both he and Lee collapsed together.

LEE AND I WERE LOADED INTO AN AMBULANCE, but first the medics had to give her a shot of something strong to overcome her refusal to leave the scene. The old guy, who turned out to be Ernest, Ben's farm manager, regained a semblance of self-control. Shrugging off attention, he moved across the yard to confront the mess smoldering in the hole that was the house basement. When he passed the Buick, he doubled up his fist and slammed it into its side.

"That had to hurt," I said to myself. "People do crazy things when they're agitated."

Lee and I were taken to a small hospital in a nearby town that didn't seem to be Ratchford. Other than being sopping wet from the ditch water, I was fine, just experiencing a sense of non reality. Lee, however, lay on a gurney for hours, as out of it as anybody could possibly be.

Toward morning, in answer to my phone call, Cousin Emily showed up with clean clothes. Together, we got Lee dismissed and pushed into the car. At Emily's house, we packed her into bed.

We decided that I'd go on over to Ratchford later in the day, after I'd had a couple of hours of sleep and a shower, and she'd get Lee to the doctor for a sedative prescription and general advice.

A few hours later, one of Emily's kind neighbors gave me a lift out to the Deckard farm to get Max. I didn't want to go back there, oh my god I didn't want to go back there, but Max couldn't be deserted. If I waited too long, I thought, there was a chance that everyone would have left the scene and I'd be alone to look at that obscene cavity where Ben's farmhouse had stood.

Once, a few short weeks before, I'd sat in the old swing listening to ancient voices tell me stories about the land. It was nice at the time but I sure didn't want to risk hearing those voices again, with whatever new chapter they could now add.

I WAS IN LUCK and the farmyard was swarming. A bunch of responder-types were slowly combing the remaining debris while sightseers watched. I wondered why, since there surely wasn't a single object in the pit that hadn't disintegrated into dozens of charred pieces.

Standing beside a Ratchford farmer type, I imitated his gloomy, silent stare. After I'd earned respect by doing this for a while, I asked, "What are they looking for?"

"Ah, well," came the careful reply, "they're trying to see if they can find any remains."

Ernest was still there, looking like death warmed over. When he saw me, he came over and said, "Why don't you go on into town to my house? My wife, Marilyn, was just out here and we want you and Janilee to feel welcome at our place while we get all this settled."

Forty-Four

Marilyn Weist turned out to be a real sweetheart. After sitting me down with a cup of coffee and a man-sized chunk of German *kuchen*, she showed me the Monday *Des Moines Register* with big headlines reading: "Two Prominent Ratchford Citizens Killed in Tornado."

According to the paper, Caroline Allan had stopped by Ben's farm to visit and both had ended up killed when the tornado ripped the house apart or, maybe, when the fluke fire, no doubt the result of a lightning strike, happened afterward. Two other visitors to the Deckard home had escaped unharmed, had been taken to a nearby hospital and were then released.

Lee and I weren't identified as the visitors, but there was plenty of beside-the-point conjecture. The paper said somebody had seen the well-known community leader, Mrs. Caroline Allan, out photographing wild flowers in the rain and guessed she'd stopped by the house of her lifelong neighbors, the Deckards, before returning home. Her husband later confirmed that was the case. She'd called him on her cell to mention her intended visit and tell him she'd be home soon.

The newspaper continued: the well-known state environmentalist leader, Mr. Ben Deckard, had been preceded in death by his father, the successful and well-known community leader, Karl Deckard Sr.; his mother, the well-known church leader, Marjorie Deckard, and by his brother, the well-known community athlete, Karl Deckard, Jr.

There was some more about the freak tornado, which apparently had only hit the Deckard farm and then blown itself out without doing further damage in the area.

I wanted to puke. My sister was suffering, Ben was dead, and that nasty old teacher had gone visiting at the wrong time. It rubbed me the wrong way to think of all the newspaper readers who would say, "Wow, look at this! We were pretty lucky it didn't do more damage," and then flip over to the comic page.

Instead, I was polite as nice women began pouring into the house bearing pies, cakes and casseroles. Word had gotten out that, in lieu of surviving family, the Weists' home was central to personal action on behalf of Ben.

Ernest arrived home looking anguished and worn out, and I could see from the way he and Marilyn held on to one another that they felt a tremendous loss, that Ben was very dear to them and now was gone.

Over the next few days, as I came and went in their home, my appreciation for the two of them grew. They gave a human quality to Ben's death and it needed one. The Ratchford Bank had taken over official arrangements, with some old girlfriend of Ben's getting into the action as spokesperson. Ben's attorney, who came out from Marshalltown, had showed up to handle the immediate estate questions.

Because most of the Deckard farm was intact and needed attention, Ernest was to act as farm manager until final decisions were made.

I MADE MYSELF PART OF THE FUNERAL SCENE for Lee's sake. Nothing could have gotten her out of Cousin Emily's house but it seemed as if someone had to represent her. It wasn't a comfortable role for me but I was mindful of what my mother would consider proper behavior and that helped.

The night before Ben's funeral, Lee came out to see the Weists and thank them. Some of her old Ratchford High classmates had come over earlier and asked about her, but for the most part she was out of the picture. She and Ben had been a juicy story right after the Ratchford school reunion but only the Weists, bless their hearts, had much real knowledge of the future she and Ben had planned together.

Two funerals were scheduled, the first for Caroline Allan, one on the next day for Ben.

Marilyn Weist told me there had been a problem deciding where to hold Caroline's. Caroline had been so involved for decades with all the activity stuff that had gone on at both Ratchford Congregational and the Ratchford Holy Trinity Lutheran Church that people in both institutions thought she was a member of their congregation.

When somebody thought to ask Harold Allan, he decided the honor belonged to the Lutherans, favoring it because he thought it came closer to the Dutch Reformed denomination he'd been raised in. Marilyn hinted it was probably the first time he'd had anything to decide, outside of his farm business, in 50 years of marriage to Caroline.

"What kind of person was she?" I asked the Weists. I was

genuinely curious about the old dame.

"Part of everything that's gone on in Ratchford since she came here to teach," Marilyn said, carefully.

Ernest just looked at me for a minute, then his head banged shut just as Lee's often did when she thought I was being nosy about her private thoughts. He wasn't open to any mental communication or, apparently, any discussion at all. Even though he maintained an impassive face, I could sense unusual turmoil going on in his mind.

"This man knows something about Caroline that nobody else does," I thought. "And he's never even told his wife." Actually, Ernest was someone who, in my observation, had a lot more things going on in his brain than he had ever let on. My suspicion was that he had some degree of psychic powers, an attribute he would have fought against as unbecoming to an honest Iowa farmer.

I was not surprised when, on the day of Caroline's funeral, he refused to attend. I went with Marilyn, partly out of curiosity and, again, mostly to represent Lee. After all, Caroline and Ben had died together and etiquette required some kind of acknowledgment, even if unspoken.

The sanctuary was smothering in heat and the heavy scent of carnations. Every organization in central Iowa must have sent flowers. To my astonishment, there was a casket—a very elaborate one.

I don't know how they had gone about making out which cinders were Caroline's and which were Ben's. That's a part of the way in which experts get things done that I don't mess around with finding out. But they'd evidently scraped together something, sorted it out, called part of it "Caroline" and part of it "Ben" and then divided it between two expensive boxes. Okay with me.

The obituary the minister read was the longest I've ever heard, being a regular encyclopedia of every award Caroline had ever won and every activity she'd ever engaged in. Glancing around, I noticed a bunch of women come in as a group and Marilyn whispered to me that they were present and former Ratchford teachers.

Some of them were rolling their eyes at one another and upwards toward the busy ceiling fans, taking care to cover smirks with their hands. I took this as a demonstration showing that an unspecified number of people harbored sarcastic opinions of Caroline.

Publicly, though, she was getting a sendoff that reflected what she would have thought she deserved.

Before the preacher was half-way through the obituary, I realized Caroline had to have written it herself, at some time, and formally filed it with some entity she figured would play a part in her inevitable departure. She had probably pre-chosen her casket, as well. People do that, I'm told.

One thing I was certain of: it wasn't the doing of her husband, Harold. A proper farmer of the older generation, he would have considered this kind of thing better left up to the women folks. In fact, he looked downright cheerful as he followed Caroline's coffin down the aisle after the service. As we all got up to leave, I overheard two local men making jokey remarks.

"First time I ever saw old Harold Allan smile!" one of them said to the other.

Dene Hellman

Forty-Five

BEN'S MEMORIAL SERVICE was the following day, at the Congregational church. We prepared to leave the Weist's house, not quite sure how Lee was going to manage the ordeal. Marilyn and Ernest, in their decent Sunday clothes and in their decent way, were wonderful stand-in parents to her. Lee was pale and quiet, all cried out for the time being.

"We'll be lucky to get a seat if we don't hurry," Marilyn worried. "Everybody in the county will be there."

"Will Earl Door be there?" I very carefully asked. He had been on my mind quite a bit for the last few days. When I got some time to myself, I had a lot of serious thinking to do. While it was unlikely that we'd ever renew our acquaintance, Mr. E. Door owed me an explanation or two.

As I expected, Marilyn looked at me oddly. "Not likely," she said. "He retired to Texas many, many years ago to be near family because he wasn't in very good health. Besides, he'd be over a hundred years old by now if he was still alive."

AT THE CHURCH, the board of directors of the Ratchford Bank was standing in the vestibule beside the coffin. It was topped with a single spray of white flowers and a tall woman, who seemed to be part of the bank crew, was beside the casket, alternately bawling and sneezing. She looked sharply at Lee when we walked in but Lee's eyes were cast down, unseeing. I don't think the big, polished hardwood box had any meaning for her whatsoever, and no wonder. I'm sure she wasn't assigning Ben's whereabouts to funeral home merchandise.

The board of directors was evidently waiting for everyone to arrive before marching in as the official mourning group.

"How appropriate," I thought. "Those dorks certainly should mourn. For the first time in over a hundred years, they'll be losing their hold on Deckard money." I'd heard from Marilyn that a Des Moines golf consortium had already placed a bid on the Deckard farm. It was strategically located within a triangle of large towns and, if their offer went through, little white balls would eventually roll across former pasture land and into the temperamental creek.

172

Certainly, all related financial dealings would be taken many miles away from Ratchford.

Moments after we entered the church, a big blond man came in. Spotting Lee, he walked over and put his arms around her. As he held her, murmuring something in her ear, she had a melt-down and began crying again, hard. He got out one of those big, well-ironed linen handkerchiefs that men never seem to carry anymore and wiped her eyes, then stepped back to join two older men who appeared to be talking into the sleeves of their French-cuff shirts.

"Who is that?" I muttered to Lee.

"Ivan. Not Ivan. Oh, I don't know," she muttered back.

In what was likely one of the few arrogantly masterful gestures of his life, Ernest took Lee by the arm and stalked past the Ratchford Bank people. Marilyn grabbed Lee's other arm and the four of us sailed down the center aisle to the front pew that had been roped off for the mourning bankers. Sweeping it aside, Ernest motioned Lee and Marilyn into seats. I slipped into the pew behind them, where I could keep a sisterly eye on Lee.

When the bank crew came down the aisle, they uncomfortably filled up the rest of the space in the front pews. The tall, weepy woman—who at first acted as if she was going to sit beside me—instead squeezed herself in at the end of the front pew where she had to compete for space with Marilyn's expansive girth.

The church was packed. The minister gave a nice little homily about everlasting life and a couple of people got up and said appreciative things about the kind of person Ben had been and how half the people in and around Ratchford had directly been the recipients of his kindness.

Then the big, blond guy got up and talked about how much Ben had contributed on a State-wide level, and how happy Ben had been this last month of his life at being reunited with the love of his life, his fiancé Janilee Jasper, and what the loss of that future partnership would mean to the good people of this beautiful land, this glorious State of Iowa. If, he said, the good folks of Ratchford could put aside their hesitancy about conservation issues, perhaps some of Ben's dreams could still be salvaged.

Stifled sobs came from every direction of the sanctuary. In my psychic mind, as the blond man stepped down, I could hear an audible click of voting machines.

We were not finished. The Congregational preacher said close friends would now go to the Ratchford Cemetery to see the big box positioned for burial in Iowa soil. That's not quite how he said it, but he then added that a post-burial reception would be held in the Ratchford Bank annex.

I figured we wouldn't be attending the reception part.

When we came out of the church, I could see the big blond guy off to one side shaking Ratchford hands and talking a mile a minute. Some of the folks crowding around him held up cameras and clicked away. I wondered if I'd ever hear of him in the future but guessed I would. Everybody in the USA finds out, from time to time, who's going to be trucking around Iowa next and what they're going to say.

The banker people got into big cars for the parade. Since we'd driven to Ben's funeral in Max, top up, I took my cue from Ernest's early demonstration of just who the real mourners were, muscling in behind the hearse even though I had to drive right up over the church lawn. This got us in front of a black limo that seemed to be packed with bankers. Thanks to innate Iowa courtesy, they dropped back instead of fighting me but I could make out nasty looks.

It did wonders to bring our little party of four temporarily out of our mourning mode. Ernest grinned at me and shot me a thumbs-up. Marilyn twisted her handkerchief while nervously giggling. Lee stiffened with horror but quickly acquired a look of acceptance.

PEOPLE DO CATCH ON FAST sometimes, it seems. At the cemetery everyone waited under the big awning beside the grave until Ernest established us in the front row. I sensed a few approving looks. A good many of the locals who cared for Ben were probably glad to see the money people put in their place, having suffered considerable humiliation at their hands during years of rural boom and bust.

The preacher read some scripture and there were some prayers. When it was over, a long line of Ratchford people came up to shake hands with Lee and the Weists. I stood a little off to one side, since I didn't consider myself exactly part of it, watching the people as they came forward and then moved off to their vehicles.

I especially noticed an older man in a shabby suit who stood to one side, head bowed. As I looked at him, he raised his head and our eyes met. It was Earl Door, of course. He knew that I was on to him by now and that, even if either of us had been so inclined, there was no need for words.

He bowed slightly, a courteous old-fashioned bow, then turned and walked away. I wondered if he would speak to Lee, since I was there as a go-between, but he didn't. For a moment or so, until he melted into a nearby grove of trees, I watched him pass quietly through the crowd of Ratchford people. He must have known many of them at one time and I thought it a pity that he couldn't—or wouldn't—make his presence known.

I thought to myself how there are some teachers who, thank God, never stop being concerned about their students and who will cross any and all necessary boundaries to look after the ones who need them. Ben would surely have safe passage.

Forty-Six

WE SAID GOODBYE to the Weists later in the afternoon, with promises to stay in touch. We all meant it. Lee and the Weists were one another's link to Ben and, for me, they were kind of like parents I might have picked out if I'd gotten to do my own choosing. They would be comfortable with my redneck husband, Jack, just as they were with Lee's la-de-da ways, because they were so totally comfortable with themselves.

Besides, I was determined to get into Ernest's head sooner or later and find out what he knew or thought he knew about Caroline Allan. I can't explain why I feel so driven on that subject, but unexplainable energy pushes me and I will do what it takes to find out what it is all about.

The next day, Lee and I thanked Cousin Emily for being good to us and drove to Boxville. With no words exchanged, I got behind Max's wheel and drove every foot of the way. We were silent; Lee didn't want to talk and mostly stared straight ahead, mentally driving along with me but keeping her feelings to herself.

One exception was when we crossed the Mississippi River Bridge. As I more or less confidently crossed the span, she flashed me a smile of such pride that I knew part of her was still intact and that healing would come.

ONCE WE GOT TO WISCONSIN, she withdrew to my back bedroom and took up her silent conversation with herself. She lay on the bed, shades drawn, for days. The four cats arranged themselves around her in a quiet vigil, even the 15-year-old calico who hates everybody.

Jack was sympathetic and aggravated at the same time.

"You mean," he grumbled out of the corner of his mouth, "all five of them are just going to lay in there moping, 24/7, just getting up for a drink of water or to pee?"

"Give it time," I said. I had a lot of catching up to do with business and the dogs. Besides, in some odd way, my brain felt bruised and I had to do some personal readjustment. When I had a few minutes, I shuffled the Tarot deck in an effort to find out what the future held for my sister.

The answers were pretty clear cut. She had a lot of living to do. "What is Lee going to do now?" I asked.

"*She's going back to the Carolinas and either get her old job back or find a new and better one,*" was the essence of the response.

"What happy things does Lee have to look forward to?" I asked.

"*Lee will find happiness with her children and future grandchildren,*" was the answer.

Then came the corker question. "Is Lee going to find another love to replace Ben?" I asked.

"*It won't be important to her,*" was the answer. "*She isn't going to seek a love anymore because Ben was who she always looked for and he's part of her now. Someday, a long time from now, she will meet someone who reminds her of Ben and they will share an agreeable friendship.*"

AFTER SEVERAL DAYS, Lee got up off the bed one morning and the cats nonchalantly moved on outdoors to catch up on their squirrel chasing activities. She still didn't talk much but that afternoon she wandered outside and began pulling weeds out of my overgrown flowerbeds.

The next day we went down to the Four Corners Café and got butterscotch malts.

The day after that we drove to Madison and checked out the summer clothes on sale.

Lee's real estate agent called with an offer on her house. "I'm going back to the Carolinas next week," said Lee. "When the house sells I'll look for a smaller one that has garden possibilities."

"Listen," I said. "How about coming back North just as you were planning to do? It would mean a lot to me if you lived closer."

She answered so quickly that I knew she'd considered the idea as she lay mourning. "I can't," she said. "I love the South and for some reason have come to feel as if it's where I belong. Being with Ben was the real incentive I had for moving back to Iowa—and I knew it wasn't going to be an easy adjustment." That night she began cooking dinners. I appreciated the break from that chore enough to shush Jack when he complained about having to eat spinach soufflé and vegetable quiche instead of the fried potatoes and Swiss steak he preferred.

When Lee was ready to reserve a flight from Madison to Charlotte, I told her of a decision I'd made. "You've always loved to

177

drive," I said. "I want you to take Max down to Charlotte. He brings out the free and the brave in you. When you get the money for your house you can replace him with something similar and bring him back "

She agreed with almost no arguing, a sure sign that it was a comforting idea. Then she asked me the question I'd been dreading to hear.

"Why did you come down to Ben's farm that afternoon?" she asked.

"Got a phone call from some guy suggesting you were in some kind of danger," I said, a roundabout answer but truthful.

"Who was it?" she asked, and I said the man hadn't identified himself.

"Must have been Ernest," she said.

I knew better but I wasn't going to go there. "You think?" I said.

The day before she left, we went over to Devil's Lake State Park and climbed the bluffs. Part way up a long trail, I asked, "What do you guess it's going to take to keep you going?"

"Little things," said Lee. "Learning how to get through the days by appreciating little things."

We paused in our climb to watch an eagle take off from its perch on top of a tall bluff and swoop down over the lake.

Forty-Seven

USUALLY I WALK DOWNTOWN to the post office every day. Boxville is too small to have home delivery of mail so we all have our numbered boxes in an old building on Main Street. There's a plus to that. We sometimes run into people we haven't seen for a while and Walt Everly, who has been behind the postal counter forever, is Boxville's answer to CNN. When it comes to daily community updates, he's the man.

One drizzly, rainy day toward the end of July, a few days after Lee and Max took off for the Carolinas, I put on Jack's old rain parka and strolled to Main Street. I said, "Hi, Walt!" as I walked into the post office and went over to the side where our little P.O. box is located. The preacher from the Methodist church was pulling his mail from the bigger church box.

"How are you, Maggie?" he said, all dignified. He knows what I do for a living and, like many of the proper town people, he doesn't approve.

"Staying busy, Ed?" I asked.

Tactfully, he tried to make conversation without dragging his church into it. He shuffled his mail and looked with interest at a post card.

"Well," he said, "my high school graduating class is having a reunion next month in Ohio. I've never gone to one of those and, after twenty-five years, I think it's about time. So I'm going to take a few vacation days just for myself and go over there to attend."

"Take care," I said, sticking our mail into my pocket. "These high school reunions can be life-changing!"

On the way out the door, I looked back at Ed, who was riffling absent mindedly through the rest of the church mail. While I was at it, I took a good, hard look at the aura I could see floating around his head. Whether he knew it or not, he was being pulled back to Ohio by a vague memory of someone he'd known in high school, not by a longing to reconnect with his old basketball buddies. Should I turn back and talk to him? Nah, he was an okay guy but he didn't have any respect for me and, besides, if push came to shove, maybe he'd remember the little warning I'd already given him.

Reaching home, I saw Jack, who'd been rained out of his

construction site job, making a bored face at his coffee cup. He hates that kind of day.

"What's new in the City of Boxville?" he asked, not really caring."Nothing much," I answered. "Except that the Methodists are going to be looking for a new preacher, come September."

The End

Dene Hellman

A native of Iowa, Dene has lived in North Carolina for two decades. She is a graduate of the University of Wisconsin Green Bay and has written professionally in numerous genres, including corporate publications, executive speeches, newspaper feature writing, and commercial videos. She has co-authored two books of poetry, *An Explosion of Toads* and *Swirls on a Green Plate*. She currently lives and writes in Winston-Salem, NC. She has four daughters and six grandsons.